## "One day I must find out whether or not you have any blood in your veins."

Clare stood rooted to the spot, staring after Denzil, her whole body shivering, remembering her strange dream, and the terror and the fever she had felt as his mouth moved against her throat....

D1047975

**CHARLOTTE LAMB** was born in London in time for World War II, and spent most of that war moving from relative to relative to escape bombing. Educated at a convent, she married a journalist, and now has five children. The family lives on the Isle of Man.

# Charlotte Lamb

# VAMPIRE LOVER

## Harlequin Books

TORONTO • NEW YORK • LONDON
AMSTERDAM • PARIS • SYDNEY • HAMBURG
STOCKHOLM • ATHENS • TOKYO • MILAN
MADRID • WARSAW • BUDAPEST • AUCKLAND

ISBN 0-373-11720-5

VAMPIRE LOVER

Copyright © 1994 by Charlotte Lamb.

First North American Publication 1995.

**Printed in U.S.A.**

# CHAPTER ONE

CLARE met Denzil Black the day he first arrived in town. It was autumn, the leaves turning brown, crimson and russet on the trees, the skies a deep purply blue as a storm blew up out of the west.

The wind rattled the agency window, and the lights flickered. Clare frowned, her blue eyes anxious, hoping they were not going to have a power cut; they often did during stormy weather, when power lines blew down. Well, it was closing time, anyway; she might as well go home. She got up from her desk and began putting on her coat, brushing her blonde hair out of the way.

The door from the street opened and the wind blew into the office. Clare looked round, beginning to apologise politely.

'I'm sorry, we're just closing. Could you come back tomorrow?'

She had already turned off the main lights; the room was rather dim. She couldn't see much of the man standing just inside the door, except that he was very tall, with black hair, and wore a long, dark coat which was flapping around him in the wind.

'I saw your board outside a house at the top of Hunter's Hill,' a deep voice said. 'A large Victorian house, set back from the road—is it still for sale?'

'Dark Tarn,' Clare said slowly, trying to make out his features in the shadows. All she could see was the glitter of his eyes staring back at her. 'Yes, it's still for sale,' she said, suppressing an odd shudder that ran down her back. It must be the wind that made her suddenly so cold.

Nobody wanted to buy the old house on the edge of the town. It was far too big for the average family. It could be turned into a small hotel or a nursing home but was in bad repair and would need a great deal of renovation before anyone could move into it. It had been on the house agency's books for two years now; her father would be thrilled if she could sell or even rent it.

'Well, can you show me round the place?' the stranger asked.

'Yes, certainly, would tomorrow morning suit you? At, say... eleven?' Clare casually picked up her desk diary and a pen, hiding her eagerness to make this sale. That was easy for her; she was an ice blonde, pale-skinned, even her eyes a light blue, very cool.

'I'm going to be busy all day tomorrow,' the dark man said. 'How about now?'

A warning bell rang in Clare's brain. Coldly polite, she said, 'I'm sorry, that isn't possible.'

Her father had impressed it on her years ago that it was not safe for her to accompany a strange man to view an empty house. They always made careful arrangements so that she had someone else with her on these occasions; usually her brother, Robin, these days, now that her father was semi-retired. Robin was just nineteen, a student at the local technical college, taking a course in business management, but he was large and muscular, he played rugby for the college and was a keen gymnast. Clare always felt very safe with Robin around.

'What do you mean, isn't possible?'

The curt question made her stiffen. 'We operate from nine until five-thirty, Mr...?'

'Black,' he said in that deep yet smoky voice. 'Denzil Black. Is the manager here?'

'I am the manager!' She felt his disbelief and added coldly, 'This is my agency.'

'The sign over the door says the agency is run by a George Summer!'

'That's my father, but he has retired, and I run the agency now!'

'I see.' She felt him staring at her, his eyes glittering in the semi-darkness. 'Well, Miss Summer... or are you married?'

She hesitated, feeling an odd, inexplicable, almost atavistic reluctance to tell him her name. Something about him had begun to bother her; she suddenly wanted to get rid of him as soon as possible. 'I'm Clare Summer,' she said shortly.

'Not married, then?'

'No,' she almost snapped. 'Look, I'm sorry, Mr Black, but I really can't spare the time to show you the house tonight.'

His tone was incisive. 'Miss Summer, either you want to sell Dark Tarn or you don't. I am going abroad for several months, tomorrow. Tonight is the only time I could view the house. Either show it to me now or we'll forget it.'

She hesitated, biting at her lower lip. Neither her father nor her brother would be at home yet. They had both gone to watch a rugby game in the next town and wouldn't be back for a couple of hours. She could ask her sister, Lucy, to drive to Dark Tarn to meet them, of course. Lucy would be home from work by now; she taught at the local primary school and was always home by five o'clock.

'Make up your mind,' Denzil Black said impatiently. 'I have my lawyer in the car; Helen Sherrard, I expect you know her—I wanted her to see the house too, but I don't want to keep her waiting out there much longer.'

Clare gave a faint sigh of relief. 'Oh, Helen! Yes, of course I know her. Very well, Mr Black, I'll take you over to Dark Tarn now, but I have another appointment at seven, and I can't be late for that. We'll have to make this a rapid viewing.' She turned to the filing cabinet, quickly flicked through the files until she found the one on Dark Tarn, took a set of keys from a locked box on the wall and locked up both the cabinet and the key safe again. Before she left she glanced at herself in a mirror hanging on the wall while she buttoned her dark red winter coat, which had a shawl collar and fell to mid-calf.

'Your coat is almost Victorian,' drawled Denzil Black, watching her. 'It suits you.'

It was a backhanded compliment; she gave him a dry look. 'Thank you.' So, he thought she was old-fashioned, did he? No doubt he thought he was insulting her, but he was wrong. Clare didn't object to the description at all, especially from a man like him.

Oh, he was attractive: her body had felt the magnetic pull of his attraction as soon as he'd walked in here. But Clare had learnt long ago not to trust men, especially attractive men. Life had always spoilt them; you were a fool if you got involved, you were asking to get hurt. You had to keep them at a distance, freeze them off. Clare was an expert at that by now.

She checked that her desk drawers were all locked, collected her bag and an umbrella, and walked towards Denzil Black. His face still in shadow, he opened the door into the street for her.

'I have to set the burglar alarm and lock up,' Clare said.

'I'll wait by my car.'

Clare took in the sleek grace and power of the black machine. She wasn't a car fanatic, so she couldn't guess the make of it but she didn't have to know much about cars to realise that this was an expensive luxury item. If Denzil Black could afford this car, he could afford to buy Dark Tarn, which answered one of her secret doubts about him.

When she had finished setting the alarm and locking the shop, she walked over to join him. He watched her, his stare flicking from her short, smooth blonde hair to her long, slender legs and elegant feet. Clare dressed timelessly, in simple, classy clothes which wouldn't go out of fashion in a few months. She didn't dress for men, she dressed to look cool, calm and capable, but that was not how she felt under his amused, mocking stare.

Having Denzil Black watch her like that, especially as she slid her long legs into his car, made the back of her neck prickle. She had the feeling that this man was real trouble.

Helen turned from the front passenger seat and gave her a polite smile. 'Hello, Clare.'

Clare would have liked to ask her some questions about her client, but Denzil Black walked round the car too fast. Before Clare got a word out he was getting into the driver's seat, so she smiled in a friendly way and said, 'Hello, Helen. How are you?'

'Fine,' Helen said, but Clare thought she looked rather pale. She was a woman in her early thirties with a warm, full figure, rich auburn hair and vivid green eyes. Her skin was usually creamy and flushed, but tonight she had very little colour and her eyes had a languid, almost drowsy look, as if...well, as if she had been making love, Clare thought, startled by her own guesswork.

She quickly looked away, wondering: Was Helen having an affair with her client?

Helen had acquired a reputation for being a flirt lately, ever since her divorce from Paul Sherrard, a well-known local hotelier. As soon as she had been on her own, men queued up to get her attention. You only had to date more than one man a year in this little backwater of a town to get yourself talked about, and ever since she and Paul had split up Helen had been seen around with a succession of other men. None of her relationships had lasted or seemed serious. Maybe she believed that there was safety in numbers. Or maybe she was simply in a wild, reckless mood after her divorce. She and her husband had been mad about each other once, but gossip had it that Paul had had some sort of passing fling with a guest in their hotel, and Helen could never forgive him.

The car started smoothly and shot away from the kerb. Denzil Black clearly knew the way, so Clare didn't have to give him directions. She sat back, watching his hands on the wheel. There was a faint scattering of black hairs across the back of them; they were long-fingered, deft and powerful. On one wrist she saw a gold watch glint, and he wore a heavy gold signet ring, stamped with what looked like a coat of arms.

She still hadn't seen his face, but she saw his thick, glossy black hair shine in the light every time they passed a street-lamp. His black coat had an expensive look; cashmere, she suspected, very smoothly tailored. Yes, he definitely had money.

Helen was murmuring to him in a low voice; Clare couldn't hear most of what she said, but then Helen asked in a husky, almost angry tone, 'How long are you going to be in the States?'

Denzil Black shrugged. 'A month, maybe two.'

'That long?' Helen sounded desolate. Clare frowned, sorry for her. Clare remembered a time when one man could make her feel like that; it wasn't an experience she ever intended to repeat. She had not found pain habit-forming.

Denzil Black pulled up at traffic-lights a second later, shot a backwards glance at Clare. 'If I do buy this property, Helen will act for me while I'm away.'

'I see,' Clare said. 'Do you live in Greenhowe at the moment, Mr Black?'

'No, but I've been staying just outside town, with Helen's brother and his wife, at their lovely home.'

'That's how we met,' explained Helen huskily.

Clare didn't know her all that well—they often met on business, to discuss the affairs of clients, but they didn't meet socially. Clare wasn't part of the social set, the way Helen undoubtedly was! Her family had always had money and, even more importantly, land. Jimmy Storr had inherited an old Queen Anne farmhouse with several hundred acres of good arable land a mile outside Greenhowe; he farmed while his wife ran a country-house hotel whose small restaurant had a county-wide reputation for excellent cuisine. Laura Storr was a wonderful cook, using fresh ingredients mostly produced on their own farm. They both worked hard, but they played hard, too, led a busy social life, and were very popular.

Clare's family were not in the same social sphere, which didn't bother her at all. She didn't enjoy noisy parties, or belonging to the country club; she didn't play team sports or give dinner parties. She walked and swam, read a good deal, went to the theatre, or the cinema, saw a lot of her family, and a few close friends. She and Helen Sherrard were miles apart in every way, but Clare had always liked the other woman, just as she liked Helen's brother and sister-in-law.

She had been sorry for Helen lately, too. After her divorce Helen had been so unhappy, and unable to hide it. I hope she hasn't been stupid enough to fall in love with someone she hardly knows! thought Clare, and then, in the mirror above his head, suddenly caught the glitter of Denzil Black's grey eyes. They had very large jet-black pupils which made his eyes seem dark, and heavy lids which were thick-lashed.

Even as Clare looked into the strange eyes, the lids drooped, hiding their expression from her, and he turned his head away, his reflection vanishing abruptly from the mirror.

Clare gave a start, wishing she had had more of a chance to examine his features. She couldn't help being curious about him. How did he really feel about Helen? Was he taking her to see Dark Tarn as his lawyer, or because of a more personal relationship? Was he hoping that the house might one day be their future home? Clare couldn't begin to guess at any answers to all those questions.

By now, they were out of town, in the green countryside, rapidly going up Hunter's Hill, the ancient boundary of Greenhowe. On one side of them lay the grey, wintry sea, far down below steep cliffs, and barely visible in a twilight which was fast becoming night. On the other ran pastures, grazed by sheep, the low-lying land dissected by dry-stone walls, in the distance the dark swell of the moors and hills like a crouching animal stretched out on the horizon.

Dark Tarn could be seen from a distance in almost any direction—a Victorian Gothic building with a medieval flavour, its turrets and battlements dominated the skyline for miles around.

'My God, it's creepy!' Helen muttered.

Denzil Black laughed. 'Don't you like it?' He didn't sound as if it mattered to him whether she did or not. Clare frowned. Not that it was any of her business, but she was curious about their relationship.

A moment later they came to a halt in front of elaborate ironwork gates. Clare got out and went to unlock them with a key from the set she had in her pocket. The lock was a little rusty; she struggled with the key. Denzil Black got out of the car and came to help.

'I'll do it.' His hand reached for the key, touching hers. A jab of electricity went through her; Clare jumped back.

He shot her a veiled sideways look. She felt herself go red and was furious. Why on earth had she reacted like that? He'd think she was some schoolgirl, blushing because a man came too close to her!

A second later, the lock turned with a grating sound, and he pushed the gates open.

'This lock needs oiling.'

'Yes, I'll see that's done tomorrow.' Flustered and irritated, Clare retrieved the key and went back to the car with Denzil Black walking just behind her. The wind was howling through the trees ahead of them, in the wild gardens of Dark Tarn; out of the corner of her eye she saw the man's long black coat blowing around his legs, as if he had wings and might take off at any minute and flap away into the night.

They drove slowly up the winding gravel drive, which was rutted and overgrown with moss and grass. Wild rabbits ran for cover, their white scuts showing as they shot away.

It was hard to see much of the garden, but Clare knew it was wildly overgrown with enormous rhododendrons and laurels in towering banks on either side of the drive.

The empty house loomed above them suddenly, the windows shuttered, no sign of life. Around the high turret a dark shape fluttered; a bat, registered Clare. There was a colony of pipistrelle bats living in the roof; she wondered if Denzil Black had noticed and whether or not the presence of bats might put him off. Some people hated bats, were terrified of them. She couldn't think why, as pipistrelle were quite tiny creatures only interested in devouring insects and no threat whatever to people. Clare would have loved to have some in her own cottage. She decided not to mention them to Denzil Black.

'There's no caretaker?' he asked at that moment, and Clare shook her head.

'The owner didn't want to pay for one. He's living in Australia, and has no intention of ever coming back here; he just wants to sell the house. It is still furnished, but, if you're seriously interested, we can deal with that. The furniture will all go up for auction, and you'll have vacant possession.'

'We'll see,' he said vaguely, staring up at the sky.

Helen looked up too, gave a high-pitched scream. 'Ughh...what's that?'

'A pipistrelle,' Denzil Black said softly. 'They're delightful little brown bats...hardly bigger than a large moth. I wonder if there's a colony in the roof?

There must be a lot of space under the rafters. It's exactly the habitat they love.'

He knew a lot about bats; well, it was a point in his favour. Clare smiled and in the mirror saw a brief reflection of his dark, glowing eyes.

'Do you like bats, Miss Summer?'

'Love them—I'd like some in my own place.'

'You have your own house?'

'I'm renovating an old farm labourer's cottage not far from here; I work on it every weekend,' she admitted. 'But for the moment I live with my family, during the week, in town.'

'I'm interested in interior decoration,' Helen said with her first sign of enthusiasm. 'Are you doing all the décor yourself, Clare?'

'Well, at the moment I'm mending the roof,' Clare said drily. 'And then I have to replaster the ceilings and walls. It'll be a long time before I get around to any décor.'

Helen looked horrified. 'It sounds as if the place is a total wreck!'

Clare laughed. 'It is.'

'What on earth made you buy it?'

'It was very cheap, and it was a challenge,' Clare told her as they pulled up outside the house.

'You're braver than I am, then!' Helen said, making a face.

Clare felt Denzil Black's dark gaze in the driving mirror, but didn't meet it. She sorted out the large front-door key, slid out of the car, and climbed the steps to the door. This lock turned easily enough, the door swung open with a prolonged creak, and

Clare fumbled for the light switch just inside on the panelled walls of the hall.

Light blazed from a chandelier hung high above their heads. Ahead of them stretched the arched vault of the roof, and the panelled walls, hung with an extraordinary mixture of objects—paintings, sketches, prints, armour, photographs in silver frames, weapons, the heads of dead animals mounted on wooden plaques.

The wind blew through the long hallway; a door crashed shut somewhere up above; stained-glass windows further down the hall rattled.

'It's monstrous!' Helen wailed, huddling into her coat, her pale face only just visible above the collar. 'You can't be serious about being interested in this place, Denzil! It's a tomb, not a house.'

It was cold, Clare had to admit, and not simply because it was empty and this was autumn. The house had a deep coldness which was in the very bricks and stones of the building. She had a feeling it would never be warm, even if you lit a fire in every room.

'Central heating will soon warm it up,' Denzil Black said, opening the first door leading off the hall. 'That shouldn't be difficult to install.'

Clare could see his face now, clearly, for the first time; an austere bone-structure, a wide, passionate mouth, strong nose, those pale eyes with the glittering centres, his black hair growing from a widow's peak on his high temples. Each feature contradicted all the others; it was not an easy face to read or assess.

'I like big rooms,' he said, looking around the main reception room.

'This is certainly big,' agreed Clare.

'Big! It's enormous!' groaned Helen.

On two sides of the room windows ran from ceiling to floor, those in the turret bay having deep, cushioned window-seats. All the rooms in the house had high ceilings; from this one another chandelier hung, giving the room a party glitter. There was a wooden fireplace like the prow of a ship, the hearth dressed with Victorian Minton tiles which bore black-line medieval style pictures on their ochre background.

The furniture was old and shabby, the stuffing leaking out of Victorian chairs, the curtains threadbare, the carpets showing signs of wear and tear.

On every possible surface stood silver-framed photographs and ornaments; the walls in here were as lined with paintings and drawings as the hall had been. There were so many objects, in fact, that the effect was mind-numbing; you looked and looked until you could take in no more.

'Wonderful,' Denzil Black said.

'It's only fit for the garbage truck!' Helen complained.

Denzil Black asked, 'Are the entire contents for sale, did you say? If I buy, I'd want first pick of everything in the place.'

'I'm sure that could be arranged.' Clare would be relieved if they managed to sell a tenth of the stuff. There were a few antiques of value, but most of the furnishings were in bad repair and would sell for peanuts at auction. Clare often acted as auctioneer at sales; her father mostly did them, but when they were dealing with a large number of objects it took hours, and Dad found it tiring after a while, so Clare usually took over to finish the auction. She had learnt to price objects at sight, and had a very good idea how much money would be raised by the sale of the contents of Dark Tarn.

'Oh, Denzil, surely you can't be serious?' Helen moaned, following him as he strode on down the hall to the next room, a few curled brown leaves blowing along with him from the open front door.

Clare paused to close it, before following the other two. She found them in the gloomy servants' hall; a long, narrow room with tiny windows, a lot of dull brown paint, and walls which had once been cream-coloured, on one of which hung a row of bells labelled with the names of other rooms. From the ceiling hung ancient hooks, from which hams and herbs had once hung, and a broken laundry pulley, which had been used to suspend washing high above the heads of the servants as they sat around the long, well-scrubbed deal table.

'It's so dreary!' Helen said, staring around the room with unhidden distaste.

'All it needs is a coat of varnish, a pretty wallpaper, some white paint—it will look wonderful! This dresser must be the same age as the house,' Denzil said, running a finger along the dust piled up on the shelves which held rows of plates and bowls and jugs.

'It is,' agreed Clare. 'Some of the china is quite good, too. A lot of it's Victorian, and it will fetch excellent prices at auction.'

'I may well want to keep it all,' he said.

'Oh, my God!' Helen groaned. 'It would be like living in a museum!'

Eerily, on the flat top of the dresser, stood a bowl of long-dead flowers, their skeletal shape dusty and dry, wreathed in cobwebs, among which was the mummified body of a spider.

Helen stared at it, dramatically shuddered, wrapped her coat around herself, and gave Denzil Black a reproachful stare. 'It's like the *Mary Celeste* in here! I keep expecting the owners to come back from the dead. I can't take any more—I'm going back to the car. Hurry up before I freeze to death!'

She stamped out, her high heels clattering along the tiled floor of the hall. The front door creaked open, slammed shut with a booming, echoing sound.

'I'm afraid she doesn't like the house,' murmured Clare.

'Well, she won't be living in it,' Denzil Black drawled, and Clare's blue eyes flickered thoughtfully.

Oh, wouldn't she? Well, bang went one theory. Obviously he had not brought Helen here to see her future home! Did she realise that?

Clare didn't think she did. Helen had been showing an almost proprietorial attitude towards him; Clare was convinced their relationship was not purely professional.

She met Denzil Black's glossy-pupilled eyes and saw sardonic amusement in them. He had been watching her, reading her thoughts. A faint pink crept under her skin.

'I wanted her to advise me on the property value,' he said.

At once, Clare told him, 'I think the house is a bargain, considering its size and the very large amount of land that goes with it.'

He gave her a dry look. 'Well, you would say that, wouldn't you? I was hoping Helen would give me a neutral point of view. Shall we go upstairs and see the rest of the place?'

The house seemed even bigger upstairs, and emptier, too. Every movement they made echoed, their footsteps on floorboards creaked. It was freezingly cold, too.

Clare would have liked to follow Helen out of here, but she kept reminding herself of the percentage the firm would get from this sale, so she followed Denzil Black around from one bedroom to another, forcing herself to make bright, encouraging comments.

He must be mad even to consider buying it, she thought, staring at the four-poster bed hung with ancient, tattered dark red curtains, which dominated the main bedroom. The oak shutters were closed across the high windows, there was only one faint lamp beside the bed, and the light reflected in a narrow Gothic-arched oak-framed mirror hanging on the opposite wall. That would probably sell well at auction. It was small enough for modern houses, and perfectly in tune with the current taste for art nouveau.

As she stared at it, Denzil Black looked round and followed her gaze.

'That's charming,' he said at once. 'I'll certainly want to keep that.'

He had very good taste. Curiously, she asked him, 'What do you actually do, Mr Black? What's your job?'

'At the moment I don't have one.' He shook a curtain, watched the dust fly up from it. 'But don't worry, I'll be paying cash for Dark Tarn, if I buy it. There'll be no problem about money.'

That was not what she was thinking about. Her curiosity about him still unsatisfied, she asked, 'Where do you live at present? I mean, apart from staying at Jimmy Storr's hotel?'

He gave her a dry, sardonic look. 'Los Angeles.'

Her eyes widened. She hadn't expected that. 'Really? But you're not American, are you?' He had a faint accent of some kind, admittedly, but she hadn't pinned it down as American.

'No. I was born in Scotland, not that I remember anything about it. I left there when I was two years old. I lived in Manchester until I was twenty-one, but I spent a succession of very good holidays in Greenhowe in my late teens.'

'Oh, that's why you've come back?'

He looked amused. 'That's what you wanted to know, was it? Why I wanted to move to Greenhowe? Well, in answer to your next question, I've lived in California for years now, mostly around Los Angeles and Beverley Hills.'

'Beverley Hills?' She stared at him, couldn't keep back the question, 'You aren't in the film business?' She laughed as she asked, expecting him to shake his head.

'Yes,' he said, though, calmly.

'Oh.' Clare was incredulous. 'Doing what? You're not an actor?' But he could be, she thought; he had the looks for it, and, even more, the charisma; she could imagine how dynamic he would look on film.

'I did some acting, many years ago—I was an extra once. But I wanted to be on the other side of the camera. I've worked at a number of jobs in the industry—stills photographer, cameraman, set designer. My ambition was to be a director, and I finally got there, but I'm out of a job at the moment, and wanted to get away, which is why I'm back in Britain.'

'And you picked Greenhowe because you remembered it better than Scotland?' she worked out, and he nodded.

'I had very happy memories of Greenhowe; summers on the beach, walks across the moors. A travel agent booked me into Jimmy Storr's hotel, so here I am.' He dusted his hands with a handkerchief, grimacing. 'This whole house is filthy.' He leaned against the wall, those dark eyes cool and steady. 'Well, let's talk business, Miss Summer. The price is ridiculous, considering the state of the house, as I'm sure you realise. I shall have to spend a fortune renovating it before I can move in. I'll tell you what I'm prepared to pay, and you can talk to the owner and let Helen know his decision. I won't bargain. I'm making one offer and that's it. If he turns it down, I won't want to discuss the matter any further.'

Clare watched him calmly, nodding.

He named the price he was prepared to pay. It was far less than she had hoped and her blue eyes hardened.

'Well, of course I'll put your offer to my client,' she said flatly. 'But I doubt if he will be ready to agree to such a low amount.'

'How long has the house been on the market? Some years, isn't it? Empty houses deteriorate quickly; this one is falling to bits. In another two years the roof will go, kids will smash the windows, the garden will be completely wild, and then it won't take long to become a total ruin.'

He was right, but Clare wasn't admitting it. 'I'll talk to my client,' she said in a cold, remote voice, and turned to walk back down the stairs and out of the house, with Denzil Black behind her.

The storm was deepening outside, the wind howling around the house like a wolf. There was a crash of thunder and a white zigzag of lightning split the sky, then the chandelier lights flickered and went out, plunging the whole house into darkness. Clare was halfway down the wide, elaborately carved staircase, and she stopped dead, blind in the unexpected blackness.

Denzil Black was right behind her. He put a hand on her shoulder, and she jumped about ten feet into the air. 'Have you got a torch?'

'In the car,' she told him, her voice a mere thread of sound.

He sighed. 'Never mind, I can see in the dark. Give me your hand.' His fingers slid down her shoulder to her arm, down her arm to entwine around her hand; Clare would have liked to pull away—he had the strangest effect on her—but she didn't like being here alone with him in the dark, she urgently needed to get out of this house, so she let him lead her down the stairs.

When they got to the car Helen was standing beside it and ran towards them, flung herself at Denzil Black, close to hysteria. 'All the lights went out! There was a terrible flash of lightning...didn't you see it? The storm's right overhead; I was afraid it would hit the car, then I saw this flash...and the lights all went out. I called and called—didn't you hear me? How could you leave me out here all by myself in the dark, all this time?'

'You shouldn't get so upset!' soothed Denzil Black, his head bent over hers. 'I can hear your heart beating like a drum!' He lowered his head, Clare thought she saw him kissing Helen's neck and hurriedly looked away, very flushed. They might remember she was there! She didn't want to be an audience for their lovemaking!

Helen gave a long, ragged sigh, winding her arms around him. 'Oh, Denzil...'

'Shh...you're safe now,' he soothed. 'We'll drop Miss Summer off and then I'll take you home. Get back into the car now. You'll feel better when you're warmer.'

Languidly, Helen obeyed, settling down into her seat without another word. As Clare got back into the car she noticed that Helen had her eyes shut and was apparently half asleep.

As they drove away from Dark Tarn Denzil Black asked, 'Where do you live, Miss Summer?'

'Just around the corner from the office, in York Square. You probably know it; it's a Georgian square behind the Town Hall.'

'I know. Very handsome houses; they've been well preserved, too. Has your family lived there long?'

'My father was born in the house; I've lived there all my life. It's a warm, family house; we love it.'

'But you're planning to move out, all the same, when your cottage is fit for occupation?'

'There are quite a lot of us,' Clare unwillingly explained. Why did he ask so many questions? 'I'd like to have more room to myself.'

'You have a lot of brothers and sisters?'

'Two brothers and a sister,' she said. 'And there are only four bedrooms between all of us. Dad has one to himself, so do my brothers, because Robin is a student, and needs somewhere private to study, and so my little brother, Jamie, has the tiny boxroom to himself, and I share a bedroom with my sister.'

'How old is she?'

Helen stirred resentfully. 'Do stop asking her questions, Denzil! You sound like a TV chat show host!'

He laughed, but Clare saw his long hands tighten on the wheel, the knuckles briefly showing white, and suspected he hadn't liked being pulled up by Helen in that way.

For a while he drove in silence, then they reached town and began to navigate a way through the one-way-street system until they came to York Square. The early nineteenth-century houses ran on each side of the square with well-cared-for gardens in the centre, set back behind green-painted Victorian railings. It gave the square a feel of the country, especially in summer, when the trees and bushes were in full leaf, and there was a scent of flowers on the air.

'Which house?' Denzil Black asked and Clare leaned forward to point.

'That one, by the street-lamp, with the holly trees in the garden.'

He parked under the street-light, and Clare politely thanked him. 'I'll let Helen know my client's decision as soon as possible,' she promised. 'Goodnight, Helen.'

Helen sleepily murmured, 'Night.'

Denzil Black got out of the car and came round to open Clare's door. 'Thanks,' she said, avoiding his hand as he tried to help her out. 'Goodnight, Mr Black.'

Before she could walk away, the front door of the house opened and in the yellow light from the hallway a girl was outlined, her face framed in a cloud of long, smooth silvery fair hair.

'Who's that?' Denzil Black's voice had altered. Clare shot a look up at him and frowned, not answering.

There was a long silence, while the girl began walking towards them.

'Is that your sister?' asked Denzil Black slowly, and Clare answered him in a chilly voice.

'Yes.' She wished Lucy hadn't come out just now. Clare was intensely protective towards her sister, and she was also deeply intuitive; her intuition told her now that it wouldn't be a good idea for Lucy to meet Denzil Black.

'Goodnight, Mr Black,' Clare said, willing him to get back into the car and drive away.

He didn't. He stood there, watching Lucy stroll down the garden path towards them, his face intent. Clare gritted her teeth. She would have loved to know what he was thinking.

As Lucy came into the circle of lamplight at the gate she paused, smiling, her oval face taking on a shimmering quality. She wasn't wearing make-up, and yet her skin was perfect, smooth and clear.

She and Clare shared the same colouring, yet there was an immense difference between them. Clare knew that she herself was very attractive, and men always liked the look of her, but Lucy was, quite simply, beautiful.

More than that, she had a mysterious radiance which was partly due to her very fair skin, the long, flowing golden hair framing her face, her eyes, which were a deeper blue than Clare's, and partly to a childlike nature.

Perhaps because her family had always spoilt her, Lucy had never quite, it seemed to Clare, grown up, yet she was so lovable that it didn't matter. Lucy was kind-hearted, loving, generous. Clare had always worried over her, afraid that some day someone would hurt Lucy. It had been a great relief to her when Lucy got engaged to someone who, she knew, would never make her little sister unhappy.

'What a fabulous car!' Lucy said as soon as she was within earshot. 'It's a Lamborghini, isn't it?' She gave Denzil Black a fascinated look. 'Is it yours? Hello, I'm Lucy, Clare's sister. We haven't met before, have we?'

'I'd remember if we had,' he said, his jet pupils glittering as he took the hand Lucy held out to him. He bent and kissed it and Lucy gave a startled gasp, then laughed.

'You aren't French, are you?'

He laughed. 'I had a French grandmother—does that count?'

'Of course. I knew it—you look French!'

'I'd be here all night if I started talking about the way you look!' he murmured, and Lucy blushed and laughed excitedly.

Clare was so angry that her teeth hurt. 'Helen is in a hurry to get home, remember,' she told Denzil Black tightly.

He gave her a dry look, then glanced towards the car, and at that moment Helen leaned forward and banged peremptorily on the window, gesturing.

'Denzil!' they all heard her call crossly.

He gave her a wave, looked down at Lucy, smiled, his eyes glowing and dark-centred.

'I'm afraid I have to go, and I'm leaving for the States tomorrow for a couple of months, but I'll be back—we'll meet again.'

He got back into the car, the engine fired and the Lamborghini moved off with a dulcet roar.

'I want that car,' Lucy said dreamily. 'Isn't it heavenly? And him...what did he say his name was? Denzil something? That's a very unusual name; I've never met anyone called Denzil before. Is he your new boyfriend, Clare? You've never mentioned him—have you been keeping him a secret? He's as gorgeous as his car. I've never seen anyone like him—where did you find him and why is he with Helen Sherrard? Tell me all about him.'

'He isn't my boyfriend. I barely know the man; he's just a client.' Clare tried not to lose her temper, but her voice was raw and she felt Lucy staring at her in surprise. It was very unusual for Clare to show temper.

'What's the matter?' Lucy asked uncertainly.

'Oh, never mind. Let's get indoors, it's cold,' Clare said, walking towards the house, very fast.

She had not liked the acquisitive way Denzil Black had been looking at Lucy. She barely knew the man, but she did not like or trust him.

Despite the temptation of her own share of the purchase price on Dark Tarn, she hoped the owner would turn down Denzil Black's offer for the house. Then, maybe, Denzil Black would go away and find somewhere else to live, and she needn't worry about what might happen next time he met her little sister.

# CHAPTER TWO

THE owner, however, accepted Denzil Black's offer at once. 'So we've managed to get rid of that white elephant at last!' Clare's father said, hearing the news, then gave her a shrewd look. 'You don't look overjoyed! Got doubts about the buyer's ability to pay?'

'No,' Clare said grimly, not bothering to explain the doubts she did have, and went to ring Helen Sherrard.

'Oh, that's wonderful!' Helen said in lack-lustre tones, barely managing to sound alive, let alone delighted by the news. 'I'll make sure you get the deposit immediately, and start proceedings rolling.'

'This offer isn't subject to a surveyor's report, is it?' That was unusual, but Denzil Black had not mentioned the idea of getting a surveyor in to look at the house.

'No, Denzil says he'll take it, whatever the condition. He's going to do a lot of work on the house anyway, and he has taken that into account in the offer he made.'

'He's getting a very good bargain,' said Clare, almost wishing he would make difficulties so that she could talk the client into not selling to him, although that would be cutting her nose off to spite her face, and she wasn't usually that childish. She was surprised at herself. 'If he's paying cash, then it shouldn't take long to complete the transaction.'

'No, I'm sure it won't,' said Helen slowly. 'I just have to do the land search, to prove title.' She gave an audible sigh.

'You sound so tired, Helen—are you working too hard?'

'Not really, but I get so bored with work; mine isn't exactly a thrilling job, you know. And I'm missing Denzil. He seems to have been away for months, although he only left a few days ago.'

Clare was doodling on her desk pad, frowning. 'How long did you say he would be away?'

'Oh, a couple of months, at least—he hopes to be back in time for Christmas, but he isn't sure he'll make it now, it seems.'

'Too bad,' Clare said indifferently. 'Well, let me have the deposit, then, and I'll make sure my client gets in touch with his solicitor too. Bye, Helen. Talk to you again soon, I expect.'

A couple of days later she met Helen in the High Street and was shocked by her pallor. 'You've lost a lot more weight, Helen. I think you ought to see a doctor! There must be something wrong with you.'

'Oh, don't fuss!' Helen snapped. 'You sound like my mother!'

'Sorry to do that,' drawled Clare, laughing. 'Was Mr Black pleased to hear his offer had been accepted?'

Helen's face tightened. 'Yes. Did you see the picture of him in the Sunday papers?'

'Never read them,' said Clare. 'Haven't got the energy to do anything on Sunday mornings except sleep late. Why was he in the newspapers?'

'He got some award or other. There was a big photo of him with the star of the film, that one who was a serious actress, did a lot of plays on Broadway before going into films. She has long black hair and a fabulous figure. Deirdre something-or-other, I think; she's half Mexican, half Irish.'

'What a combination! I know who you mean, though,' said Clare, frowning. 'It wasn't Deirdre, it was Bella something or other. I saw her last big film, the vampire film—it was pretty way out, if you ask me! The sex scenes almost burnt the celluloid they were printed on.'

'That's the one,' said Helen, palely smiling. 'That's Denzil's last film.'

Clare's eyes opened wide. 'You're kidding? He made that?' It gave her a new idea of Denzil Black. She couldn't remember ever seeing a sexier film.

'And from what they said in the papers this Sunday, he and Bella what's-her-name are having an affair!' Helen said huskily, almost as white as paper. She turned on her heel to walk away, stopped, swayed, and crumpled up. Clare was too late to catch her. Before she understood what was happening, Helen had fallen sideways and hit her head on a lamp-post.

A crowd gathered, of course. Clare knelt down anxiously and looked at the wan, shadowed face in its frame of rich auburn hair. 'Helen? Helen, are you OK?'

'She's fainted!' someone in the crowd said.

'Knocked herself out,' someone else insisted. 'I saw her do it; she hit her head on that lamp-post. Drunk, most likely; she looked drunk to me.'

'Send for an ambulance! She needs to go to hospital; she's out for the count,' somebody said, and a shopkeeper leaned forward.

'I just did. They'll be here any minute.'

Helen's lashes were flickering. She sighed through lips almost as white as her face. Clare almost caught the word she said. She was almost sure Helen had said, 'Denzil...'

Clare didn't know whether to be sorry for her, or furious with her, or just furious with Denzil Black. Any woman who let a man reduce her to this state deserved a good slap, she thought, watching the other woman bleakly.

The ambulance arrived a moment later, siren wailing. The crowd cleared enough to let the men through with their stretcher. They took a look at Helen, asked, 'What happened?'

A babble of voices tried to answer.

Clare cut through them coldly and efficiently. 'She fainted, and managed to hit her head on that lamp-post while she was falling.'

The voices stopped, and people stared at her. She was well-known in town; nobody argued openly, although she heard a few whispered comments from those who preferred to believe Helen had been drunk.

She went to the hospital with Helen, and rang Helen's mother from the waiting-room. 'They're keeping her in here tonight; they want to do some tests on her. They think she could be anaemic; apparently her blood-count was very low, and so is her blood-pressure.'

Helen's mother sounded terrified. She was a small, delicate woman, and very highly strung. She often seemed to Clare still to be grieving for her husband, who had died a couple of years ago. Tears came easily to her, and she wore either black or grey most of the time.

'Oh, no; you don't think...they don't think...it might be...? Her father died of cancer, you know——' She broke off, obviously close to tears now. 'Clare, if anything happened to Helen... I've been so worried about her; she has been terribly pale lately, and she never has any energy. That was how it happened to her father. She used to be the life and soul of the party. Well, you remember what she was like before the divorce, Clare! I know you weren't a close friend, but you've known Helen for years; she was always full of fun. But over the last couple of months she's been fading away, and yet the doctor could never find anything wrong with her.'

Clare's blue eyes had an icy sparkle. Well, she knew what had been wrong with Helen lately, and there was nothing the doctor could do to help that pain. 'Will you ring Paul and let him know?' she asked Joyce.

'Paul? Oh, do you think I should tell him? After all, they are divorced; I expect he has someone else by now.'

'Well, they were married for a long time. I'm sure he'll be concerned about her.'

'Oh . . . Clare, I . . . Clare, couldn't you?' gabbled
Joyce. 'If you rang him, it would be so much easier.
I mean. . . I don't like to interfere. . . Helen wouldn't
thank me; she might be furious with me for doing
it.'

Clare sighed. 'I hardly know him, Joyce!'

'Please, Clare . . . would you?'

Clare gave in, her face grim. She rang Paul
Sherrard at his hotel and was put through to his
office. His secretary answered breathlessly,
sounding very young and faintly scatty.

'Mr Sherrard's office. Oh, yes? Miss Summer?
Was it important? Well, I don't know if he's . . . I'll
see if he's free . . .'

Paul's voice appeared on the line a second later.
'Good morning, Clare. How are you?'

'I'm fine, Paul, but I'm ringing from the hospital—Helen is here, and they're keeping her in
overnight. She may be seriously ill; they aren't sure
yet. I thought I ought to let you know.'

'What do you mean, seriously ill?' Paul asked
curtly. 'What's wrong with her?'

'I've no idea, Paul, but she looks terrible. I just
thought I should let you know. I've rung her
mother; she was very upset. I wish I could get the
doctors here to be frank, but they won't commit
themselves.'

'Oh, won't they? We'll see about that. I'll be there
in half an hour,' Paul said, and rang off.

Clare stayed at the hospital until Paul and Helen's
mother arrived, almost at the same time, and then
she had to get back to the office, which had been
closed all this time.

She rang the hospital later that day, but there
was no further news, other than that Helen was in
no danger, was conscious again, and would be in
hospital for some days. Clare sent her flowers and
a get-well card. She visited her the next afternoon
and found her sitting up against banked pillows,
still pale, still listless.

'They say I can go home at the weekend,' Helen
said. 'After these tests. They think I'm anaemic.
I'll have to drink blood, like Dracula!' She laughed.

Clare didn't. She was too horrified by how ill
Helen looked; by the dark shadows under Helen's
eyes and the thin, restless, frail fingers. It was a
relief to find that the illness was nothing worse than
anaemia—no doubt that would be a huge weight
off Mrs Storr's mind—but Clare kept remembering
Helen's look of pain as she talked about Denzil
Black and his sexy actress. That man had a lot to
answer for! 'You're beginning to look better,' she
lied.

Helen brightened. 'Do you think so? They say I
mustn't go back to work, I must rest for a few
weeks, and I'm going to my brother's place, to stay
with him. Paul thinks I should go abroad after
Christmas; he's going to Majorca to the apartment
we owned over there, and he suggested I came too.'
A faint flush crept up her cheeks. She gave Clare
a defiant look, looked away quickly. 'Well, we were
married for years. Nobody will think anything odd
about that.'

'Of course not,' said Clare. 'I think it's a brilliant idea.'

She smiled at Helen warmly. If Paul took her away she would soon forget Denzil Black, and maybe Helen and Paul might even get together again for good, not just for a holiday?

Very flushed, Helen said, 'Oh, and Johnny Pritchard is dealing with Dark Tarn, by the way.'

'I wasn't worried about it,' Clare said coolly. 'It can wait.'

'Oh, no,' Helen said, sounding shocked. 'Denzil is in a hurry.'

'Never mind him,' said Clare. 'You just look after yourself.'

Over the next few weeks she seemed to be busier than usual. This was usually a dead time of year. People didn't buy and sell houses in winter; spring was when their minds turned to moving home. But that winter Clare was very busy. A firm had recently built a large block of luxury apartments overlooking the harbour, and, failing to sell half of them, was eager to rent them out rather than leave them empty. They gave Clare the job of finding tenants, and for a while she was constantly driving possible clients out to the apartment building, showing them round, and dealing with their rental agreements.

As she was out of the office so much her father came in to help part-time, but she still had a lot of extra paperwork to do.

One evening in late November she was working at her desk after all the other shops had closed when the phone rang.

Grimacing, she answered. 'Hello?'

'You sound bad-tempered.'

A jab of shock went through her, but she pretended she hadn't recognised his voice. 'Who's speaking?' she asked distantly.

He laughed. She flushed.

'Listen,' he said, 'I need to have a team of men look over Dark Tarn to recommend how it can be modernised without losing its atmosphere. Will you see that they have the keys for a day? My architect is Bernard Atkins. He'll be in touch this week.'

'Very well, but nothing can be done until you actually own the house, of course!'

'I realise that. How long do you think it will be before the contract is ready for signature?'

'A week or two.' She paused, then, her voice chilling even more, asked, 'I presume you know Helen is very ill?'

'Yes, I had a letter from her, explaining. If I'm back in time before she goes off to Majorca, I'll go and see her.'

'I shouldn't,' Clare said quickly. 'She needs complete rest; she isn't having visitors.'

'She'll want to see me,' he said with a soft inflexion that made Clare shiver.

'Maybe she would,' she bit back. 'But it wouldn't be good for her!'

His voice even softer, he said, 'You don't like me much, do you, Miss Summer?'

'I don't know you well enough to have an opinion one way or another!'

'When I get back, we must do something about that!' he murmured, and she bit her lip.

'I must go, Mr Black—I'm very busy, I'm afraid. I'll make sure your architect gets the keys. Goodbye.'

Clare put the phone down hurriedly before he could say anything else and sat there staring out into the dark, empty street, feeling a hot pulse beating in her throat. She put a nervous hand up to it, pressed down into her flesh and felt the leap of blood under her fingertip.

Snatching her hand down, she angrily told herself not to let the man get to her. He was on the other side of the Atlantic, and she hoped he would stay there for a very long time, but when he did get back Clare had no intention of getting to know him any better!

She went home an hour later and wasn't surprised to find that nobody had cooked the evening meal yet. They were all supposed to do it in turn, but in practice it was more often than not Clare who ended up doing the cooking. Clare's father did the shopping most days, but cooking wasn't something he enjoyed or was good at, nor were any of the others. Robin and Jamie thought cooking was 'for girls' and Lucy, although always willing to do it, often drifted off into daydreams and forgot.

That evening she wasn't even home yet, and only walked in halfway through the meal. 'Oh, terrific! Sausages and onions,' she said happily, sitting down in her usual chair, and helping herself from the large dish in the centre of the table.

'You were supposed to cook tonight, Lucy!' her father reproached her.

Lucy gave a groan. 'Oh, no, I knew there was something I'd forgotten! Who cooked it, then?'

'Who do you think?' enquired their father wryly, and Lucy gave Clare a guilty look.

'I'm sorry, Clare, I honestly forgot! It went clean out of my head! I'll do it next time it's your turn; when's that?'

'Tomorrow.'

'Right, I won't forget.' Lucy looked down at her food. 'There wasn't a letter from Mike again today. That's nearly ten days. I hope he isn't sick.'

'It's probably the post,' Clare said quickly, watching her sister anxiously.

Lucy was delicate and sensitive, and easily hurt, and it had been a relief to her family when she met Mike Duncan a year ago, while she was still at college. Mike had been doing postgraduate research at the same college; he was four years older than Lucy, and had had some work experience before returning to do his postgraduate work.

Quiet, steady, friendly—the whole family had liked Mike at once, and been delighted when Lucy got engaged to him, but then Mike had taken a job in Africa for a year in a teacher-training college there. He had insisted that he and Lucy postpone their marriage until he returned, and again the whole family had agreed with him, although from time to time Clare had her doubts. It had been the sensible decision. Lucy was very young, and a year wasn't an eternity, but Clare realised that Mike's absence was making Lucy restless.

He had been away now for six months; he would be back in the spring, for their wedding. He wrote all the time, and sent recorded audio tapes of messages too; but it wasn't the same as having him there and Lucy was lonely and often bored.

'As long as he hasn't met someone else!' Lucy said, pretending to laugh, but not acting very well.

Clare and her father exchanged glances, but neither said anything. They knew what the other one was thinking. What if Lucy's fears proved true? The tremor of her lips told them how badly she would be hurt.

'Can I have some more chocolate mousse? Oh, did I tell you what I want for Christmas? I made a list, to help you, save you time trying to guess what I want,' Jamie said, only interested in his own concerns.

'Don't even mention Christmas!' Clare thought of all the work the festive season entailed and groaned aloud. She would have to make some lists of her own any day, but for the moment she was putting off all idea of Christmas until she felt strong enough to cope with it.

'Eat your mousse and then you can help clear the table,' George Summer told his younger son. 'And after that you can finish your homework.'

Clare watched Jamie take another huge helping of mousse without even thinking about him. She had Denzil Black on her mind. It would take months for him to have Dark Tarn modernised—would he stay in America meanwhile? Now that he had won this big award, maybe he would be offered other jobs? She remembered him saying that he was leaving America because he hadn't been asked to make another film. What if he was? Maybe he wouldn't be moving back here at all. Maybe he would sell Dark Tarn again, once he had had it renovated?

She felt her pulse take that odd, disturbing skip again, and bit her lip. She didn't like the man. Why should she care?

December started badly: icy winds blew sleet and snow through the town from the sea, which had a chill grey look as it heaved and surged under a sky banked with dull, heavy clouds pregnant with yet more snow.

Lucy finally heard from Mike. Three letters came at once; the post was erratic from Africa, especially at this time of year. Lucy was flushed with excitement and relief, but Clare still worried. Her sister's wild mood swings bothered her. Lucy was far too volatile. Clare wished Mike were coming home sooner.

Early in the month, Dark Tarn became the property of Denzil Black, causing a flurry of interest from London newspapers and the local TV station. A camera team invaded Clare's agency and tried to interview her, but she coldly asked them to leave, and refused to answer questions. They still did an item on the news that night.

'Why didn't you talk to them? It would have been great seeing you on TV,' her brothers complained.

'Professional etiquette. I can't talk about my clients,' she said, and her father agreed.

Her brothers looked disgusted.

Clare was able to bank a sizeable share of the price. The agency had done rather better this year than she had expected, in fact; their bank statements were looking very healthy.

'I think we could afford to pay someone to help me in the office, at least part-time, now,' she told her father, who agreed.

'Then maybe you can take some time off occasionally! I hate to see you look so tired!'

'Oh, I'm fine!' shrugged Clare.

'You don't want to end up like poor Helen Sherrard.'

Clare's blue eyes smouldered. 'I won't, don't worry.' She had more sense than to let a man do that to her, especially a man like Denzil Black.

That week she saw an article in a magazine about the actress who had starred in Denzil Black's last film. The photo above the print showed her on a stretcher being rushed into a Los Angeles clinic. She had overdosed on heroin and almost died. But a 'close friend' was quoted as saying that the actress had never been the same since making Denzil's film.

'It isn't drugs, it's love,' the 'friend' said. 'She hasn't seen much of him these last months. Now that he's finished the film, he's finished with her, and he's broken her heart.'

Clare stared at the blurred photo, just able to make out the other girl's haunting dark eyes and tragic expression. Wasn't that just how Helen had looked lately? What did that man do to the women who fell for him?

That weekend, Clare got the video of the film out of the local video shop and watched it several times, fascinated both by the film itself and by the beauty of the actress. She had to admire Denzil's skill as a film-maker; the film was beautifully shot, mesmerising and very different from any film she had ever seen before. The erotic content made it too adult for her to want her brothers to see it— she watched it late at night, alone. The subtlety with which the sex scenes were shot somehow made them even sexier; a glimpse of a white thigh, the tensed muscles in a man's back, the sound of a groan did far more than all the naked writhing flesh most such films used to make their impact.

After she had gone to bed she lay in the dark thinking about the film—and about Denzil Black. Seeing the film again had made her realise that he was a clever, complex, dangerous man.

When she took the video back she asked if they had any other Denzil Black films, and was given an earlier one he had made, which she watched the next night. Again, she watched it several times, and after that she saw all his films in quick succession, trying to work out more about him from the way he made them. She had never taken so much interest in a director before or realised how much you could learn about someone from the sort of work they did. All his films had clues scattered through them, she realised, picking up on some of them over and over again.

On Christmas Eve she shut up early, just after four, and hurried through the crowded, darkening winter streets looking for last-minute presents.

She was staring into the window of an expensive lingerie shop when she felt someone halt behind her. Automatically she looked at the reflection of the street which she could see in the plate-glass shop window, but she couldn't see anyone.

'Hello,' said a voice, and she stiffened, glancing round.

An icy shiver ran down her spine as she recognised that face—the widow's peak, the sleek black hair, the piercing grey eyes, the ruthless mouth.

For a second she was unable to move, paralysed like someone in a nightmare, facing something more terrible than words could express and frozen by sheer terror. She just stood there, staring into those eyes, feeling the insistence of his will burning into her.

'You haven't forgotten me, have you?' he asked in that deep, dark voice, and she wished she could nod and say that yes, she had forgotten him—but it would be a lie and, anyway, she knew he was well aware that she hadn't.

He didn't wait for her to answer, anyhow. He went on coolly, 'What are you thinking of buying? The demure white slip, or the Victorian nightgown that buttons up to the neck and goes right down to the feet? I saw you looking at them. Why not go crazy for once and buy something sexy—like that black négligé? I can imagine you in that—wearing nothing else underneath it, of course.' His smile teased, held mockery.

Hot, burning colour rushed up her face. She blinked, breaking free of the spell holding her, her heartbeat accelerating, her breathing rough. It was like waking up from hibernation. Her whole body seemed to have been stopped for that brief time, and now it began working again. Clare was overwhelmed by a feeling so strong that it made her giddy, and then she got angry. She snapped back at him, 'I'm not buying for myself, I'm shopping for Christmas presents!'

She couldn't trust herself to talk politely. She had to get away from the overpowering effect of being near him. She almost ran towards the shop doorway.

He came with her, his long legs easily keeping pace without hurrying. 'For your beautiful little sister?'

She was sorry to hear he remembered Lucy. Grimly, she realised that somehow she had to stop him meeting Lucy again. She did not want him pursuing her sister. Lucy was vulnerable at the moment; she might lose her head over this man and get badly hurt, the way Helen and that film star had been hurt.

Clare would kill him if he hurt her sister.

'You aren't living up at Dark Tarn, are you?' she asked him, pausing just before the shop door. 'I heard that the builders weren't starting work on it before the New Year.'

'Your information is very accurate,' he said drily. 'Small-town gossip is amazing. Talking about gossip, thank you for refusing to talk about me to the Press.'

Surprised, she asked, 'How do you know that?'

'One of them told me. Their interest seems to have died down now, but if it starts up again I'd be grateful if you would go on being discreet. I shall be working hard over the next few months; I don't want to waste time on the media.'

She nodded coolly. 'I understand. But you do use them when it suits you, I gather.'

His eyes sharpened to black points of light. 'They're a necessary evil, yes.'

'Talking about that, I gather from the Press that you won an award for your last film,' she murmured, looking down but watching him through her lashes. 'Congratulations.'

'Thank you.' He watched her, too, his face sardonic, his eyes narrowed.

'I was sorry to hear that your star hadn't been well since making the film!' Clare ventured, and saw his face tighten, the tanned skin stretching across his cheekbones, his mouth hard, his grey eyes icy, then veiled, as he looked away.

He didn't answer the implicit question. Instead, he said curtly, 'It was lucky I saw you. I've just been to your office. I want you to find me somewhere to live for six months or a year, until the house is finished. A flat would do, or some small cottage.'

Clare enjoyed saying, 'There isn't anywhere suitable on the books at the moment, I'm afraid. Why don't you look further along the coast—or how about York?'

He gave her a hard stare. 'I need to live near Dark Tarn while the renovation is going on!'

Clare's smile was chilly. 'Well, if I think of anywhere I'll let you know. Are you staying at Jimmy Storr's place again?'

His eyes flashed. 'No, it seems there wasn't room for me. Helen is staying there for the moment—

there were no spare rooms. I'm staying at the Black Boar, here, in town.'

Clare was consumed with curiosity. Obviously the Storr family had decided to keep him at a distance from now on! Hardly surprising, after what he had done to Helen.

'I'm sure you'll be very comfortable at the Black Boar,' she said with sweet iciness in her voice and face. 'I must rush. Bye.'

As she turned away she heard Lucy's voice, and her heart dropped like a stone.

'Clare! Hey, wait a minute, Clare...'

She looked round, biting her lip. Lucy was rushing across the road, dodging hooting cars, skipping round a bus while the bus-driver bellowed furiously at her.

Breathlessly Lucy gabbled, 'That was lucky...I only just caught sight of you...can you lend me ten pounds? I've run out of cash, and I haven't got my cheque-book on me. I'll pay you back with a cheque when we get home.'

'Yes, OK.' Clare hunted hurriedly in her bag, produced a bank note. 'Here you are.'

If by hurrying she had hoped to stop Lucy noticing Denzil Black she was soon disappointed. Lucy gave him a polite look, then did a double-take and flushed bright pink.

'Oh! It's Mr Black, isn't it? Hello. I read all about you in the newspapers after we met last time; I couldn't believe I hadn't recognised you, but the idea of a famous film director turning up in Greenhowe is so unbelievable it never entered my head, and Clare never said a word.'

'Your sister's very discreet,' he murmured, his mouth wry, giving Clare a sideways glance she ignored. 'I don't want a lot of media interest at the moment.'

'No, of course, I quite understand. You aren't living at Dark Tarn yet, are you?' asked Lucy eagerly.

'No, I'm looking for somewhere in town to move into temporarily,' he told her. 'If you can think of anywhere——'

'In town?' Lucy tried desperately to come up with a suggestion. 'A house, you mean? Couldn't Clare find you a place?'

'Unfortunately not,' he said.

Clare didn't say a word.

Lucy's eyes lit up. 'I know! I have a friend with a very large house which has been turned into flats. She might have a place to rent at the moment; would you like me to find out if she could take you?'

Clare watched him and sensed he wasn't very enthusiastic about this idea.

Slowly, he asked, 'These flats are independent? I mean, they have their own front doors?'

'Oh, yes. They aren't very big—just studio apartments, actually—one large room and a small bathroom.' Lucy gave him a glowing smile. 'It won't hurt you to look at it, if one is available, will it?'

He laughed. 'Right.'

Lucy looked up and down the High Street. 'Where's the nearest phone kiosk? There's one in the post office; I'll go over there. If Jenny has a flat unoccupied I'll take you round there now and you can look the place over. Wait here, I won't be a minute.'

As she darted away Clare said angrily, 'I don't think this is a good idea. That sort of arrangement is always full of difficulties.'

'I agree, but I don't want to spend the next few months living in a hotel,' he murmured. 'Unless you can come up with something else I may have to take your sister up on her offer. She's delightful, by the way, as well as being extraordinarily beautiful. I love her cheekbones and that wide, full mouth; I like that look—warm-blooded, full of life.'

Clare bit her lower lip. She was suddenly very afraid for Lucy; she didn't want to see her sister ending up the way Helen had, the way the Mexican-Irish actress had done—lifeless, pale, their lives wrecked.

'Of course, there is my cottage,' she said slowly.

'What?' He stared, his brows lifting as he followed her inconsequential remark. 'The one without a roof?'

'I got the roof on weeks ago! In fact, most of the structural work is finished, and so is the central heating and rewiring.'

He looked amazed, his eyes sharp and piercing. 'You did all that yourself?'

'No,' she said with impatience. 'I had some help from a builder I know, who did me a good job very cheaply because I put so much business his way. I've had a very good year financially, and I'm so busy I hardly get time to work on the cottage at the moment. I've even managed to get a few of the rooms redecorated, and the plumbing is fine now.'

Denzil Black drawled with amusement, 'Is that why the builder apparently can't start work on Dark Tarn—because he's too busy working for you?'

'It isn't the same builder! My man is much cheaper; he has a very small labour force—well, just him and his brother, actually. He probably wouldn't be able to handle a job as big as renovating Dark Tarn. It would take the two of them years to get all those jobs done.'

'Well, when can I see your cottage? Now?'

'Now? It's a bit late now, it's nearly dark. I'm afraid it will have to wait until after the Christmas holiday.'

'I don't want to wait. Take me there now.'

'I can't...' she began, then saw Lucy hurrying back. 'Don't tell my sister I'm letting you have my cottage,' she said urgently. 'I...don't want her to know...for...for private reasons I can't discuss.'

Denzil Black's piercing grey eyes skewered her; she felt he could read her thoughts in her face and looked away, very flushed. She didn't want him telling Lucy because she didn't want Lucy knowing where to find him, or dropping in on him, whenever the mood took her. She wanted Denzil Black out of the way, as far from Lucy as possible.

'I won't tell her, if you take me out to see it tonight,' he said softly.

Clare could have hit him. 'That's impossible!'

He shrugged. 'Up to you, of course. So, I tell Lucy?'

She looked at him with fury. 'Are you black-mailing me?'

His eyes glinted with unrepentant amusement. 'If you like. In my world you learn to do deals using any weapons that are available. You have some-thing I want; I can see you don't want your sister to know what you're up to, for some reason I won't speculate about. I'm simply offering a bargain—well?'

Lucy was only feet away. Clare had to think fast. Pink and furious, she nodded, in the end.

'Oh, very well. OK. It's a bargain.'

'Come and pick me up at the Black Boar in an hour,' he said, and before she could refuse Lucy breathlessly arrived.

'Jenny flipped. She said to come on over right away. There are two flats, just studio apartments, but they're on the top floor, away from everyone else; you can have either of them, or both of them. I'm afraid there's no lift, and obviously there are a lot of stairs...'

Clare watched his heavy frown, his shake of the head. 'A lot of stairs? No, I'm afraid that's out of the question—thanks for taking so much trouble for me, Lucy, but I shall have to turn that idea down. Never mind, I'll find somewhere else. I must go now. See you both around, no doubt.'

He was gone before Lucy had time to take on board the fact that he was walking away. She turned a disappointed face to Clare.

'Oh, dear. Jenny will be as sick as a parrot that he isn't coming. She was so thrilled. She's a film buff, and thinks he's wonderful. When I rang off she was going to rush around making the place look wonderful.'

'You had better ring her at once and explain, and save her the trouble,' said Clare.

Lucy sighed heavily. 'I suppose I'd better!'

'See you,' Clare called after her as her sister walked back to the post office. Clare went in the opposite direction. She would have to get her car and leave before Lucy came home, or she might find herself answering questions she didn't want to answer. She walked fast, frowning angrily.

Now she was committed to letting Denzil Black use her cottage for as long as he chose! That was the last thing she had wanted. Somehow he had outmanoeuvred her and got his own way. Clare had a sinking feeling that he always did. Well, in future she was going to keep a very close eye on him. He wasn't doing that to her again.

# CHAPTER THREE

CLARE'S cottage was only half a mile from Dark Tarn. Victorian, built of flint and stone, with a grey slate roof, it had been put up by a local farmer for his shepherd, close to the pastures where the ewes had grazed while they waited to give birth in the cold months of early spring. The little house had originally been very basic: two rooms and a scullery downstairs, two rooms upstairs. There had been no bathroom, not even an indoor lavatory. Some years ago there had been a disastrous fire at the cottage, and for a long time before Clare bought it the house had stood empty, decaying. The roof had gone, the windows had been boarded up, wallpaper had been peeling off walls, and some of the floorboards had had worm in them. She had been able to buy it for a song, then she had taken the place apart and put it together again the way she wanted it.

'Interesting!' Denzil Black murmured, standing in the sitting-room looking around the white-washed stone walls, considering the original local slate fireplace, which had survived the fire intact, the few scattered pieces of furniture which Clare had bought very cheaply at auctions. 'Not exactly cosy, but interesting, especially as a sidelight on your taste!'

Defensively, she muttered, 'I haven't done the décor yet, and the furniture is only temporary, until

I get round to deciding how I want the place to look.'

'It has atmosphere. These lamps, for instance, would fit in at Dark Tarn,' he observed, his glance on a pair of Victorian oil lamps standing on a highly polished sideboard. 'They look as if they belong there.'

Clare flushed. 'They didn't come from there, if that's what you're implying!'

He turned cold eyes on her. 'I wasn't. Don't snap at everything I say. It's like making conversation with a piranha.' Clare didn't have time to react to that before he smoothly added, 'But I'm always ready to make an offer.'

She stiffened. 'What?'

'For the lamps,' he said in a bland voice.

'Oh.' Clare relaxed again. Too soon.

'What did you think I meant?' he enquired, his eyes coolly mocking as the hot colour flowed under her skin.

Again she didn't have time to answer. He then asked, 'Heating?' and she stared blankly at that. 'What sort of heating does the cottage have?' he expanded.

'Central heating runs from the stove in the kitchen.' Clare couldn't quite make up her mind whether she was imagining the double-edged remarks he kept making. Maybe she was hypersensitive today, or maybe he really was having some sort of fun at her expense? Whatever the truth, he was making her edgy, so she walked out of the sitting-room into the open-plan kitchen-cum-dining-room beyond. He followed her, stopped dead, his brows lifting.

'This is different. I almost feel I need sunglasses, it's so bright in here!'

It was a warm golden room: pine cladding on the walls retained the heat and matched the pine table and the chairs, the tall dresser hung with pieces of china Clare had acquired over the years. The window blinds were printed with shiny red apples and broad green leaves; they were vivid, cheerful, almost childlike.

'This is your taste?' He sounded disbelieving.

Clare would have liked to say yes, if only because he so obviously didn't think so, and it annoyed her that he should be right. She didn't want him to guess that much about her. Reluctantly, though, she had to admit, 'Well, actually, I let my sister choose the furniture and blinds.'

'Ah,' he said, black brows lifted mockingly. 'Lucy...who looks like a grown-up version of Alice in Wonderland! Yes, that fits.'

Clare turned on her heel and went out. 'There's only one room furnished upstairs,' she said over her shoulder.

He followed, their footsteps hollow on the new, recently varnished stairs.

'I haven't yet got around to buying carpets,' she said.

'I like all this exposed wood; it looks wonderful.'

'It will mean a lot of polishing,' she pointed out. 'I know a woman in the village who will come and clean, but she's expensive, because she has to get over here by car. She cleaned the house for me after the builders left, so she knows the place.'

'Could you fix up for her to work here one day a week? That should be often enough, wouldn't you say? This isn't a large place.'

'OK, I'll ring her and ask her to call—if you decide to rent the cottage.'

'I've already decided. I'll take it for six months.' He stood in the main bedroom, glanced around at the same bare white walls, the simple, narrow bed, the built-in wardrobe running down one side of the room. Apart from that there was only a rather lovely pink velvet upholstered Victorian chair and a free-standing Victorian mirror, both of them items Clare had picked up at sales in the county over the last year.

'I'm afraid you won't be very comfortable here,' Clare protested, still reluctant to let him rent her cottage.

He gave her a dry look. 'I'll be fine. So long as you don't mind if I make the place more habitable with a few personal things—pictures, books, a music centre.'

Clare could hardly refuse. She watched him stroll over to the window and look out into the dark garden. His long shadow climbed up the white wall and she shivered.

It made her uneasy to think of him living here, in the home she had made for herself alone; buying the cottage had been an act of daring, and she had been excited about it ever since. Her family had been startled, amused, faintly indignant when they heard what she had done. A tumbledown cottage?

What on earth had made her buy it? Why did she need a place of her own? She had a home, with her father, and the two boys. Lucy was going to marry soon, she would go off and live with Mike somewhere, and then who would run the family home, play mother to Robin and Jamie? Clare couldn't move out, their eyes reproached. They needed her.

She knew they did, and she had no intention of deserting them. Clare had a strong sense of responsibility and she loved her family, but the idea of having a private bolt-hole had been irresistible.

Whenever she needed to get away from everything she would always have this cottage to run to now—and she didn't want to find it haunted by Denzil Black. If he'd lived here first, she had a queer feeling she might.

'Can I move in at once?' he asked, and she gave him an incredulous look.

'What do you mean, at once?'

'Tomorrow?'

'It's Christmas Day tomorrow. Won't you be seeing your family?'

'I haven't got one.' His voice was terse and shut a door in her face.

At once her mind clamoured to know: were his parents dead? Hadn't he any brothers or sisters? Surely he had an aunt or uncle somewhere? How could anyone say they had no family at all?

'We haven't mentioned rent yet,' he said. 'How much a month?'

Clare hadn't thought about it, but she knew the usual rents asked for such properties, and only had to think for a second. She deliberately asked for a very high rent, still hoping to scare him off.

He nodded. 'OK. Perhaps you'll get Helen's office to draw up a contract for us to cover the six-month lease?'

'After the New Year,' Clare said, irritated because he had accepted without a blink. She should have asked for more! 'They won't be at their office until the New Year. You know, the Black Boar do Christmas rather well. You'd be much more comfortable there over Christmas than moving in here.'

'I hate Christmas,' he said curtly. 'I'm looking forward to missing it.'

Clare stared at him, dumbfounded. 'You hate Christmas? You mean you won't be celebrating Christmas at all?'

'It's just any other day to me. I'll move in here tomorrow, and spend the day peacefully arranging my books and pictures. I'll have soup and a salad for lunch, and I won't be watching TV or listening to the radio, just listening to music while I work.'

'I'm sorry,' Clare said, and his grey eyes took on that jet glitter she had come to recognise.

'If you're saying you're sorry for me, don't be. Be sorry for yourself. I shall be very happy here, ignoring Christmas. I have grim memories of spending Christmas the traditional way, and I'm certain my day will be a damn sight more peaceful and enjoyable than yours.'

Clare thought of all the work she had to do— the noise and babble of Christmas morning, herself yelling for the boys to get up, Christmas carols on the TV, which was later turned up so that the boys could hear it while they reluctantly helped her and complained at the same time, their eyes bright with excitement, the litter of Christmas-present wrapping after they had opened their presents, the barking of the dog, excited to mania by all the unusual activity, the smell of something burning in the oven as she remembered the turkey and rushed groaning to rescue it, the boys laughing and pushing each other while they laid the table, herself and Lucy serving lunch, the boys arguing over who had the turkey's wishbone, crackers exploding, leaving more debris for her to clear up, the boys laughing hysterically over the awful jokes in the crackers, her father going to sleep in his armchair afterwards while she and Lucy washed up, the boys going out for a walk in the frosty air to get rid of their surplus energy and finally leaving the house quiet for an hour so that she could collapse in a chair until they got back demanding turkey sandwiches and Christmas cake.

She looked at Denzil Black and smiled, her cool oval face filling with warmth and amusement. 'My day will be magic.'

His face changed; he stared down at her intently. 'Who are you thinking about? A man? Your lover? A woman only looks like that over a man.'

Her eyes took on a frosty sparkle; she turned away, looking at her watch with an impatient gesture. 'I want to get home, Mr Black. You may not like Christmas, but I do, and I have masses of presents to wrap, not to mention a host of other jobs to do before I get to bed tonight.'

'And you don't like answering questions,' he commented.

She ignored him, making for the stairs, her head crowded with all the different things she still had to do—vegetables to prepare in advance, and store in the bottom of the fridge; a trifle and some jellies to make.

Clare loved Christmas, but it did mean a lot of work, and it was never easy to get anyone to help. Her father, the boys and Lucy would be out tonight with the carol singers around the giant Christmas tree outside the town hall. It was a Christmas Eve tradition in the town, to raise money for local charities, and great fun. She often went along, but tonight she wouldn't have the time.

She was in such a hurry that she skidded on the polished wood of the stairs and tumbled forwards.

She might have had a nasty fall if Denzil Black hadn't been quick-witted. He grabbed her coat and hauled her back against him, his arm going round her waist.

Shock made Clare's heart hammer against her breastbone, her eyes darken. For a second or two she stood there, immobile; held close to him; hearing her heart beating right through her body, hardly aware of anything else.

He bent down, and she felt as if he swooped on her from a great height, while she was helpless, unable to move. His cheek touched hers, his skin cold, smooth. Then his lips moved against her neck and she shuddered as they parted, his mouth opening against her skin as if he was going to bite her.

But all he did was ask, 'Are you OK?'

The down-to-earth question broke her out of her trance. Trembling, she pulled away from his grasp, took the last two steps down the stairs, saying, 'Yes, thank you,' huskily, over her shoulder at the same time.

She hurried to the front door and Denzil Black followed casually, moving without any of her haste.

Clare was deeply relieved to get back into her car and drive away. She would be even happier to get rid of her passenger once they reached town. Being alone with him was a nerve-racking experience.

As they drove along the town streets, coloured fairy-lights swaying from gaily lit shop to gaily lit shop above them, in the wintry wind, Denzil Black looked at her drily. 'Look at all those shops with their phoney snow and Christmas trees! Christmas has just become a big sales drive. It no longer has any religious meaning.'

Clare shot him a cold, sideways look. 'Not for you maybe. But my family always go to church. We'll be at midnight mass tonight. We always go to midnight mass on Christmas Eve, it's our favourite service of the year. It's a sung mass. Lucy is in the choir, so are my brothers. The music is always brilliant.'

'Don't tell me... guitars and rock music!'

The scornful sound of his voice infuriated Clare. 'No, the Christmas music is always traditional, Christmas carols or old Latin hymns, or classical— we have a wonderful organ. Tonight, Lucy says, they're singing Mozart and Palestrina.' She broke off and slowed, waving a hand to the left. 'There's the church now. We're very proud of it; it's one of the finest in this part of England.'

Denzil Black leaned forward to stare at the high medieval building, climbing up against the night sky, a bell tower, a vaulted roof, grey flint and stone walls, with a small green churchyard around it behind Victorian iron railings, turf growing around the ancient tombstones, shadowed by even more ancient yew trees.

'Why don't you come along tonight and hear the singing?' Clare invited, and saw him frown.

'I don't think so, thank you.'

'Scared?'

He shot her a look, eyes narrowed. 'What would I be scared of?'

'Christmas getting to you,' she said softly.

His mouth twisted, his eyes glittered. 'Maybe. And what are you afraid of?'

She drew a startled breath. 'I'm not afraid of anything!' she denied, but she felt herself flushing.

His voice was mocking. 'No? I had the distinct impression you were afraid of me, while we were at your cottage.'

She stiffened. 'Well, you were wrong. I'm not afraid of you, Mr Black, just wary of you. I've seen the effect you have, I know what you are, and I've no intention of being one of your victims.'

'One of my victims?' His features tightened, his eyes dark with anger. 'What the hell does that mean?'

They had reached the Black Boar. Clare drove up to the main entrance and pulled up.

'Here you are, Mr Black,' she said, her head turned away from him.

He didn't get out. He sat there staring at her averted profile. After a minute he said harshly, 'I'm not sure what you think you're talking about, but if you're thinking of Bella Declan it wasn't me who ruined her life, it was drugs. I got her into a clinic, but she walked out again; she wasn't ready to fight her addiction. Maybe she never will be. She was abused as a child and it went on for years. Bella is a very sick girl; the drugs are her way of coping with memories she can't face. You shouldn't believe everything you read in newspapers, Miss Summer. They usually exaggerate, and quite often they print outright lies.'

'But she was in love with you?'

His voice was impatient. 'She may have thought she was, but drug addicts live in a fantasy world. You can't believe a word they say.'

Clare turned her head and gave him a look of burning scorn.

Their eyes met. He turned dark red.

'Don't look at me like that!' he bit out. 'You know nothing about me. What makes you think you have the right to pass judgement on me?'

'I didn't say a word. Do you mind getting out of my car? I have a lot to do tonight. I'm in a hurry, even if you aren't.'

He didn't move. In fact, he seemed deliberately to relax, leaning back in the seat, half turned towards her, his head propped on one hand while his eyes moved over her in a slow, lingering stare that made her intensely self-conscious. 'Your hair's like moonlight; *clair de lune*'s the French for moonlight, isn't it? Is that why your parents gave you that name? Was your hair that colour when you were born?'

'I think my mother just liked the name Clare,' she said shortly, the hairs on the back of her neck prickling. He had such strange, brilliant eyes and the will behind them had a force which disturbed her deeply. 'Would you please get out of my car, Mr Black?'

'There's a vanload of my personal belongings up at Dark Tarn, locked in the stables,' he drawled. 'I want to move that out to your cottage and unload it all, in the morning. Could I have the keys of your cottage now, please?'

Clare hesitated, then reluctantly put a hand in her pocket, produced the keys to her cottage and handed them to him. As he took them his fingers brushed hers and she had to fight not to shiver visibly. His skin was cold, she told herself; that was all. It wasn't because his touch had any effect on her.

'Thank you.' A cool gleam of mockery lit his eyes. 'I'll even wish you Happy Christmas. I hope you enjoy the holiday as much as I will.'

'Thank you,' she said gravely. 'I'm certain I'll enjoy it far more. Like most things, you get out of Christmas what you put in!'

'You think I deserve to spend Christmas alone, is that what you mean?' He laughed. 'Look, wait here a minute, will you? I want to get something— I'll be back in a second.'

He was out of the car before she could get a word out. Startled, she watched him run through the swing doors of the old pub. Now what was he up to? Clare looked at her watch impatiently. She wanted to get home. She had already wasted too much time on Denzil Black.

As she thought that, he came loping back and got into the front seat again. Clare looked enquiringly at him. What had he gone to get?

He showed her a second later, holding it up above her head.

Clare looked up, instinctively, saw the green stalk, the green leaves, the pearl-like berries, and stiffened. Mistletoe!

'As you seem to see me as some sort of pagan, this is one tradition I'm happy to observe,' he murmured, and swooped down on her.

His mouth touched hers. Clare felt her lips burn; the kiss was over in a second but it left her feeling weak, breathless, in shock.

While she sat there, dazed and silent, Denzil Black got out of the car without another word.

Clare felt so odd that she didn't drive away for a minute, but then another car turned in behind her and hooted for her to move off. With a start, she blindly switched on the ignition and started the car, drove away and almost had an accident turning out into the main road right in front of a bus. Luckily, it was going so slowly that the driver had time to brake and stop before he hit her.

Horrified, Clare pulled herself together, made a gesture of apology to the other driver, and drove on home, shaking.

She was glad to have so much to do that evening. It was safer than thinking. Every time she did she felt her mind whirl giddily. She couldn't believe what had happened inside her when their mouths met. It had been an earthquake. Clare was still having after-tremors.

Not that anybody seemed to notice. Her family were getting ready to go out to sing carols.

'We had take-away Chinese, don't worry about us,' her father reassured her. 'Did you manage to find Mr Black somewhere to live?'

Clare looked at Lucy.

'I told Dad I thought that was where you'd gone,' Lucy explained innocently. 'I knew you wouldn't leave the poor man living in a pub all over Christmas!'

'Yes, I found him a place,' said Clare offhandedly.

'Where?' Lucy's face was eager. Clare watched her with uneasiness.

'A new place which came on the market the other day. Out of town, not too far from Dark Tarn.'

'Maybe we could help him settle in. He probably needs help, a man all on his own,' said Lucy softly.

'He doesn't need any help, he's perfectly capable and if he has any problems he can afford to pay people to do the job for him!' Clare looked at the clock in the hall. 'You're going to be late!'

'She's right, come on!' squawked Robin.

They all ran. They would be coming back later with the rest of the choir to have Christmas Eve supper before going to church in time for midnight mass. For the moment, though, Clare could relax and enjoy a tranquil evening cooking and listening to music.

She would be hearing carols in church later, so she put on her favourite Mozart piano concerto, No. 23, and began quickly to put together a huge lamb and vegetable hotpot in the oven for supper. It could cook slowly while she made the mince pies. She made them in big batches, some of which the choir would doubtless eat.

In the cold pantry which opened out of the kitchen and was unheated, cool in summer, bitterly chill in winter, she soon had a row of creamy trifles, their tops scattered with multicoloured sugar strands, and orange, red and green jellies like quivering jewels in glass bowls, standing on the marble counters running round the long, narrow room.

The whole house had a Christmas scent: the frosty outdoors smell of holly and ivy and pine cones, picked days ago by her father and the boys and put up along the picture rail, around the balustrade, across the windows, with glittering tinsel twined in with it, and foil chains in red and gold. The smell of food permeated the house, too, rich and exotic and exciting, dates and walnuts, raisins and pineapple, brandy and mincemeat.

They had dressed the house for Christmas as they always did: chains and swags decorated every room, Christmas bells hung here and there from the ceiling, and their Christmas tree stood in the bay window of the living-room, deliciously scenting the air with pine, and dropping thin sharp needles on the carpet which she had to hoover up every morning. But Clare didn't mind. It was so beautiful, shimmering with glass balls and other ornaments, a silver-painted peacock with a tail of iridescent blue feathers, a small robin made of feathers, chocolate Father Christmases and snowmen hidden among the branches, a fairy on the top of the tree, and winking on and off the dozens of electric fairy-lights which the family had collected over the years.

She sat down with a cup of coffee, in an arm-chair in front of the fire, gazing at the tree through half-closed eyes, just one table lamp switched on so that the rest of the room lay in soft shadow. The others would be back soon. She was very tired, but with that deep physical weariness which was not uncomfortable. She yawned, stretching out lazily, her mind wandering. Minutes later she had her eyes shut and was close to sleep.

Suddenly Denzil Black came into the room, his familiar black shadow falling across the walls, en-gulfing her. She had never realised before how tall he was—his head seemed to touch the ceiling, he was as thin as smoke, twisting upwards. Her blood ran cold, then hot. She couldn't breathe, let alone speak, and a languid dreaminess made it im-possible for her to move.

She gazed at him, struggling to break free, get up. He stared back at her, a strange smile curling his mouth, his pale grey eyes hypnotic, his will beating down all her resistance. Her lips began to burn as if he was kissing them again. She felt a terrible weakness. He seemed to float across the room silently, then he was bending over her and Clare could not move.

His mouth slowly came down while she watched it, languorous, feverish, wanting to feel it touch her.

But he didn't kiss her lips. His mouth swooped on her throat; she felt his lips part, hot and insistent on her skin. An icy coldness seemed to pierce her. The blood in her veins seemed to be flowing towards her neck, towards his mouth; her life was flowing into him. She was fainting, sighing with something between horror and intense excitement, her eyes closing again, the darkness overwhelming her.

Somewhere a door slammed. Clare started violently—had she been asleep after all? The door of the sitting-room was open and light fell from the hall across the room. With a jarring shock she saw Denzil Black framed in the light, standing just inside the doorway, watching her.

Clare shuddered, as hot as fire and yet at the same time icy cold. Had it happened? Or had she dreamed it? Or was she dreaming now? Was it going to happen? Would he float across the room and...?

Then behind him she saw Lucy and the boys, laughing, faces flushed with cold and excitement, and her father, and the rest of the choir crowding in behind them.

'Merry Christmas, Clare!' someone called.

'Did we wake you up? Oh, what a shame,' said someone else.

'We thought you'd have supper ready. Come on, Clare!' Robin said, grinning at her. 'We're all starving!'

'Come in here, everyone,' Lucy said, switching on the central light, and the room filled with brilliance, dazzling Clare, as she got up out of her chair. The choir piled in, laughing and talking, getting as close to the fire as they could, some of them kissing Clare, exchanging Christmas greetings with her.

She didn't look at Denzil Black but she felt him watching her, and her profile took on a marble curve, cold as the weather outside. What was he doing here? How had he managed to join them, wangle an invitation?

'Denzil heard us singing as he was out walking, and came over to listen, and stayed for ages; he was our best audience,' Lucy said, looking at him with over-bright eyes, a moist bloom on her lips. Clare's antennae prickled in alarm. 'So Dad invited him to come back with us to supper,' Lucy said. 'There's plenty of food, isn't there?'

'Of course,' Clare said stiffly, her skin chill as she watched her sister smiling at him. From the minute he saw Lucy outside their home Clare had been afraid of this—she didn't want Lucy within miles of him, but how did she keep them apart? She could see already that her sister was not going to listen to any warnings.

'Need any help?' offered her father. 'Boys, come and help your sister. Lucy, you look after our guests; get them drinks, make them comfortable.'

'I made some hot punch; Robin will bring it at once,' said Clare, hurrying off to the kitchen.

The punch went into the microwave for a brief reheating, then Robin took it away, sniffing appreciatively. 'Mmm...smells gorgeous...what's in it? Can I have a glass?'

'It's mainly fruit juice spiked with spices, but it has some wine in it, and a little kirsch—of course you can have some. It won't hurt you, so long as you don't drink too much of it.'

'Can I?' asked Jamie, following his brother, with two wicker baskets filled with sliced French bread.

'One glass only, Jamie!' Clare called after him as she watched her father, wearing oven gloves, carefully lifting the huge earthenware casserole dish in which her hotpot had cooked. 'That isn't too heavy for you, is it, Dad?'

'I'm fine,' he assured her.

She had already laid out a buffet table with cutlery and plates and paper napkins. She looked around to see what else had to be carried through to the sitting-room, and at that moment someone else sauntered into the room, his eyes bright, a coaxing charm in his face.

'Hello, Clare. Can I help?'

Clare tensed in disbelief. 'Hal! I didn't notice you with the choir. Are you in town for Christmas?'

Three years ago she had been in love with Hal Stephens, and had believed he loved her too, until he had suddenly married someone else in a hasty civil ceremony, and immediately moved away from the town to live in York with his new wife.

He had written to Clare but had only posted the letter the night before his abrupt wedding, so that Clare had actually heard the news from a neighbour, who had been heavily sympathetic yet at the same time avid with curiosity as she'd watched Clare's unguarded face.

It was another couple of days before Hal's letter had arrived, explaining that he had had to marry the other woman because she was expecting his baby.

Clare found it hard to remember now exactly how she had felt at first. Anguish and disbelief had been succeeded by merciful numbness. She had gone through life for months like an automaton, barely knowing what she was doing or saying, simply surviving. In time she had got over the whole thing, but it had left her very wary, a little cynical, distinctly cautious where men were concerned.

Only later did she realise she had had a lucky escape. Hal's letter, with its self-pity and self-justification, took that long to sink in—he wasn't in love with his new wife, he had written; he had had a brief affair with her while she was on holiday in Greenhowe that summer, because Clare was always too busy, and he was lonely, and now Stephanie was pregnant and he was trapped, but it was still Clare he loved.

Clare had been sorry for his wife later, once she could think clearly again. What sort of marriage could it ever be when Hal felt like that, talked like that about his wife? Clare would hate to know that any man talked like that about her!

Later, Clare had heard that Stephanie was nearly thirty, and not exactly pretty, but that her parents were wealthy, with a large, thriving business, and had given Hal a good job as sales manager after he married their daughter, so he had not done badly out of his bargain.

'I've been singing with the choir, and your father insisted I came along,' he said to her with a smile which didn't really doubt his welcome, in spite of how he had treated her three years ago.

Hal was spoilt, had been doted on by his mother all his life; he thought he could always talk a woman round when she was angry, and no doubt he could, where most women were concerned.

Not Clare, though. She looked back at him coolly, her blue eyes clear and derisive. She had fallen for his charm once. Never again. She had his number now.

'I said I thought you might not want to see me, but he said it was all forgiven and forgotten, and, after all, it is Christmas...' Hal's blue eyes were bright with optimism. He was blond and smooth-skinned, with boyish good looks, and far too much charm. He had learnt to rely on it. She wondered how he would manage once he was middle-aged and no longer had the charm or the boyish looks.

'Are you back in town for Christmas with your parents?' She knew his mother and father had spent last Christmas with him and his wife and their little boy. Mr Stephens ran the local hardware store; he had met her in the street one day last spring, and talked endlessly about his grandson and how well Hal was doing. He was oblivious to what his son had done to her, but his wife always looked embarrassed when she met Clare.

'That's right, and when I walked along past the Town Hall and saw the choir singing I couldn't resist joining them. It brought back so many happy memories.' He looked down at her, sighed.

'Clare . . . it's so wonderful to see you. You're even lovelier than I remember. I've never forgotten you— you haven't forgotten me, have you, Clare?'

'I haven't forgotten that you're married, with a child, either,' she said icily. 'Go back to the others, Hal. Leave me alone.'

He caught her shoulders, excitement flushing his face. 'In a minute, Clare. Just give me one kiss first!'

She was about to push him away when someone else got hold of him and hurled him across the room.

'You heard her! Get out of here!'

Clare was speechless with astonishment. She stared at Denzil, her blue eyes wide and startled.

Hal hit the wall by the door with a resounding thud. His handsome face flushed with temper, he stared at Denzil, his hands screwing into fists, and took a step back towards them.

'Don't even think about it!' Denzil advised softly.

Hal stopped in his tracks as though picking up a note in Denzil's voice that alarmed him. He visibly hesitated, then glared, muttered under his breath something like, 'Not worth the trouble!' and was gone.

'Was that specimen the one who put you into cold storage?' Denzil drawled, watching her. 'I knew there had to be someone. With a woman who looks like you, there had to be a reason for the permafrost I met every time I spoke to you.'

Bitingly, Clare said, 'And of course it couldn't be anything to do with you yourself! If I didn't swoon the minute I saw you, I had to have something wrong with me!'

He looked amused. 'Something like that. I guessed you'd had a bad experience some time, but I must say I'm disappointed in your taste. What on earth did you ever see in the guy?'

Ice in her voice, Clare said, 'I've been asking myself what women ever see in you. There's no accounting for taste.' She picked up a large jug of cream and put it into his hand. 'Take this in to the others, will you?'

He didn't obey, just looked at her through half-lowered lids, smiling. 'Don't I get a word of thanks for saving you the trouble of slapping his face?'

'Thank you,' she said distantly.

He laughed. 'One day I must find out whether or not you have any blood in your veins.' He walked away with the jug. Clare stood frozen on the spot, staring after him, her whole body shivering, remembering her strange dream, and the terror and fever she had felt as his mouth moved against her throat, and her blood beat in wild response to him.

# CHAPTER FOUR

IN THE New Year, Clare's business was at a stand-still during the dead months of January and February. Few people thought of moving house in winter, which was tough on house agents, as she said to Johnny Pritchard, the solicitor dealing with most of Helen's work while she was off on pro-longed sick leave.

Johnny was sympathetic. 'What's bad for you is bad for me,' he agreed. 'I get a lot of my income from you people! But I'm lucky, I have wills to fall back on—a lot of old people tend to die in winter, and as an executor of their wills I do get some nice fees.'

He was a nice man, in his early thirties, fair and thin, with friendly hazel eyes. His marriage had broken up some years ago and his wife had re-married after their divorce. Johnny lived with his mother in a flat on the seafront. The local gossips said his mother had caused the divorce, but she had always been very pleasant to Clare, who had known her for years.

'Mother said the other day that we must have you to dinner soon,' Johnny said. 'When could you come? This week?'

Clare hesitated briefly, then smiled at him. 'That would be nice—how about Wednesday?'

Mrs Pritchard made her welcome, had cooked a very special meal for her, insisted that Johnny play the piano for them both after dinner. He was good; not quite good enough for a career as a concert pianist, as he regretfully insisted. Clare enjoyed the evening, and invited Johnny back to dinner at her own home a week later.

'He's so quiet!' said Lucy later, grimacing. 'What do you see in him? I suppose he's quite eligible— he must earn a lot. But honestly, Clare! He's about as sexy as a bath-towel.'

Clare didn't bother to argue. She liked Johnny. Not enough to be serious about him, but that was none of Lucy's business.

They had heavy snowfalls during the first weeks of the year. Snow piled up on pavements, trees were crystal fountains, and the sea had a pale, angry look, reflecting the cold sky.

'I hope the heating is good in this place Denzil is renting,' said Lucy one chilly Friday morning at breakfast, her bright eyes inquisitive. 'Where is it, by the way?'

'I forget exactly,' Clare lied, and got a disbelieving look.

'Oh, come on, Clare! You never forget properties you've handled. You know, it must be very lonely for him in a strange town, after living in Hollywood.' Lucy sighed enviously. 'Think of it! All those parties, meeting all the famous stars; it must be wonderful.'

'And maybe it wasn't. Maybe it was the prospect of a little loneliness that brought him here,' Clare said drily, thinking how much she would hate to live somewhere like Hollywood. Country life was far more her style. 'And anyway, why are you so interested in another man when you're supposed to be engaged to Mike?'

Going red, Lucy snapped back, 'Being engaged doesn't mean I can't have any other friends, does it?'

'Not men like Denzil Black! He's labelled "Handle with Care", Lucy!'

Lucy giggled. 'I thought you didn't fancy him! You sound as if you find him absolutely fascinating!'

Clare scowled, and Lucy jumped up from the table. 'Oops... look at the time, I'd better hurry. See you tonight. I might be late. I've got a staff meeting after school, to discuss the spring pageant we're planning.'

Clare watched her go, her face worried. Lucy's interest in Denzil Black was disturbing. If she got involved with him the gossip was bound to get back to Mike. This was a small town. You couldn't keep secrets.

That was how she knew that the builders had finally begun work at Dark Tarn. It was their most famous local house; everyone was excited by the thought of it coming back to life after having been empty for so long.

A week later, Clare was locking the office for the night when a car slowed beside her and Denzil Black called out, 'I'll give you a lift home.'

Clare shook her head. 'No, thank you, it isn't far to walk.'

'Get in!' he ordered, opening the passenger door.

She saw some people she knew on the other side of the road, all ears. There was always an audience following your every move in this town. If she walked away and Denzil followed her in his car, kerb-crawling and arguing with her, speculation would be rife.

Flushed and resentful, she realised she had no option. She got into the car and Denzil drove off.

'Don't ever do that to me again!' she whispered fiercely without looking at him.

'Do what?' he asked, all innocence. 'Offer you a lift? What's so wrong with that?'

She gave him a bitter look. 'You should have driven off when I refused, not gone on pestering me in front of all those people!'

He laughed. 'Why do you care what they think?'

'This is a small town. I don't like being talked about.'

His mouth twisted cynically. 'Oh, you'd get used to it, if you had to. One grows another skin or two.'

She looked sideways at him. 'How many skins have you got?'

He smiled without looking at her. 'I lost count long ago.'

She suddenly realised that they were not taking the turning to her home. 'Where are you going?' She sat upright, her body tense in every line.

'I thought we might have dinner somewhere out in the country—I've discovered a quiet little country inn with an amazingly good chef.'

'I have a date! Please take me home.' She fought to keep panic out of her voice, tried to sound icy and remote.

'A date?' His head swung towards her. 'With a man?'

'Yes, not that it's any of your business. Would you please turn round and take me home? I don't want to be late.'

The car slowed, his face in profile now, hard, unreadable. 'I had the impression there was no man in your life.'

'Then you were wrong,' she said with a savage satisfaction she couldn't explain even to herself.

'What's his name?'

She didn't answer. He turned his dark head again to look sharply at her, eyes glittering. 'I asked . . . what's his name?'

'My private life is my own concern.'

'It isn't the guy who was pestering you at your Christmas Eve party?'

'Hal?' she said, startled. 'Of course not! Hal doesn't even live here any more; he was just home for Christmas.'

Coolly he murmured, 'Good. You know, I was surprised by what I overheard. I wouldn't have thought you were the type to get involved with a married man.'

Very flushed, she snapped, 'He wasn't married when I knew him.'

'I see,' he said slowly. 'He married after you broke with him? Which of you ended it? You or him?'

Clare was disturbed by his curiosity. She didn't want him taking an interest in her, especially in her love-life. 'Would you stop asking questions and take me home, please?'

He shrugged and turned the car round, headed back towards her home without haste. Clare unclipped her seatbelt as he pulled up outside the house, but his hand shot out and caught her wrist.

'What about this guy you're seeing now? How long have you known him? Is it serious?'

Clare icily met his probing stare. 'What makes you think you have the right to ask? What if it is serious? What's that got to do with you?'

'Is it?' he insisted.

'Yes,' she lied, and saw his eyes flicker, his brows black and level over them.

'Why won't you tell me his name? He isn't married too, is he?'

'No, he isn't. And his name's Johnny,' she snapped. 'Now, will you let go of me?'

For a moment she thought he wasn't going to; she felt nerves jumping under her skin, a sense of danger. Their eyes fought. Fire flew between them. The tension was intolerable. She thought she might scream out, but at last he let go, and Clare immediately leapt out of the car and walked away without looking back.

That was important. Not to look back. Not to let him think he had reached her in any way at all.

She hadn't lied to him. She had a date, with Johnny Pritchard, who was taking her out to a new Greek restaurant which had opened in town that winter. Clare sighed as she got ready. Johnny was so nice. Why couldn't she think about him as often as she thought about Denzil Black, who was a million miles from being a nice man?

She didn't want to think about him at all. She tried not to, when she was awake, but he showed up in her dreams disturbingly often. She kept having the strange dream she had had on Christmas Eve; she didn't know what on earth it meant but it recurred over and over again during that long, cold winter. It was always the same: she was alone in a shadowy room and suddenly Denzil was there, floating towards her silently, his eyes glittering in the firelight. It was how she felt that really worried her—the languid fever, the restless eagerness with which she watched him and waited helplessly for his mouth to swoop down against her lifted throat. As the icy needles pierced her she would sometimes wake with a wild moan of pleasure wrenching at her, and then she would lie in the darkness, trembling and dismayed.

She began to be afraid to go to sleep.

Clare didn't actually see anything of Denzil Black for weeks, but driving past Dark Tarn some time in February she noticed signs of activity—scaffolding around the roof, vans parked on the drive, piles of building materials left scattered outside the house, men with mugs of tea in their hands standing contemplating the weather, which had become milder that week after a thaw which had left many places along the coast flooded.

Lucy was rarely home during those weeks. The pageant meant lots of rehearsals after school and little free time for Lucy. At least, to Clare's relief, Lucy seemed to have forgotten Denzil Black. Lucy never mentioned him now. Come to that, she wasn't talking much about anything. Lately she hadn't read any of Mike's letters out at breakfast, or talked about her plans for the wedding, scheduled for around Easter. When Clare suggested that they ought to start making firm arrangements Lucy got agitated and refused to discuss it.

Even their father noticed that Lucy was very quiet and withdrawn. 'She's pale, too,' he said, frowning anxiously. 'Do you think she's working too hard? She puts in far too many hours of overtime on this pageant.'

'That's probably what it is,' agreed Clare. 'I'll have a word with her.'

Over breakfast the following morning Robin looked up from the magazine he was reading and said excitedly, 'Hey! It says here that Denzil Black is going to be making a film in England later this year—that explains why he's living here!'

'Does it say what the film's about?' asked their father.

'It's a novel by one of the Brontës,' Robin said. 'I've never heard of it. *The Tenant of Wildfell Hall*—do you know it, Lucy?'

'Yes, it's by the third surviving sister, Anne; it's about a married woman who runs away from a drunken husband,' said Lucy, not even looking up from the letter she was reading. Clare was relieved to see that she had lost interest in Denzil Black, and she had a better colour this morning. Her cheeks had a healthy flush. Maybe there was no need to worry about her?

'I'm taking my car in to be serviced,' Lucy reminded her as they were all about to leave ten minutes later. 'Can you follow me, pick me up from the garage and drive me on to school?'

'OK. I'll drop off Robin and Jamie first. See you at the garage.'

It gave her the opportunity she wanted to talk to Lucy, especially as she saw when she arrived at the garage that Lucy's flush had gone, she was pale again.

But Lucy flared up as soon as Clair started to talk. 'I'm perfectly OK! There's nothing wrong with me. Stop nagging!'

Clare was taken aback by her reaction. Soothingly, she said, 'I'm not nagging, Lucy. But Dad and I are worried about you. You're working too hard. You'll make yourself ill, and it isn't long before your wedding now, remember.'

Lucy turned on her, actually shouting, face tense, eyes all pupil, glittering and hostile. 'I'm fine, absolutely fine. Leave me alone!'

It was such a shock that Clare drove on in stunned silence until they reached the primary school where Lucy taught. She pulled up and Lucy got out of the car, slamming the door as she walked away without even saying goodbye or thank you.

What on earth was wrong with her? Clare was about to drive off when the headmistress walked past and greeted her warmly.

'How are you, Clare? You look a little pale. So does Lucy lately, but she's been working so hard, and doing a great job with the pageant! Isn't it thrilling that she has managed to get so much help from Denzil Black? It's really good of him to be so generous with his time, a famous man like him!'

Shock made Clare numb, but she managed to make some trite, polite reply, before driving slowly away.

So that was it. No wonder Lucy was pale and edgy, living on her nerves; that was how he made women look. Clare recognised all the symptoms from Helen, and what she had read about the actress who had starred in his latest film. She thought of Helen's face the day she fainted in the street: the pallor, the lines of strain, the darkness in the eyes, the shadows under them.

This morning, at breakfast, when Robin had started talking about the rumour that Denzil Black was making a film here—why hadn't it struck her then that there was something suspicious about Lucy's offhand manner, her apparent indifference, after she had once been so fascinated by anything about him?

Clare remembered how Lucy had flushed, even though she hadn't looked up. She had noticed Lucy's colour and been fooled into thinking that she was looking better. She could kick herself for being so blind.

Now the little pieces of the jigsaw all fell into place. Her sister was secretly meeting Denzil Black on the evenings when she was supposedly working late at school. No doubt Lucy did work for an hour or so, and then slipped away with Denzil Black. Clare's teeth met in her lower lip.

Damn him! she thought, her eyes blind with anger. Why couldn't he leave her alone? She was so young. Lucy had no real experience of life outside this peaceful backwater.

That morning Clare wasn't very busy; she spent long stretches of time at her desk staring at nothing, brooding. What was she going to do? She couldn't let Lucy wreck her life. Lucy might break off her engagement, give up her job—and afterwards, when Denzil Black was bored with her, as Clare was sure he would get bored one day? After all, he always had before, with all the others who had preceded Lucy! When it was over and real life had to be faced again, with all the bitter consequences of what she had done, what would happen to Lucy then?

He isn't doing this to my sister! thought Clare bitterly. I'm not watching while her life is ruined. I've got to stop it. But how?

She went out to lunch at one o'clock. On her way to her favourite restaurant she saw Denzil walking rapidly on the other side of the road, his long black coat blowing in the wind, and her heart almost stopped. Every so often during the past weeks she had seen him like this, at a distance, and each time she felt this worrying sensation, close to terror, yet throbbing inside her like a dynamo another feeling altogether, one she refused to face, even to admit existed.

Denzil slowed his stride and turned to cross the road. Clare fled into the nearest shop to escape.

'Can I help you?' asked the woman behind the counter.

Clare looked blankly at her, not knowing what the shop sold. She had to look around to check. 'Oh...three oranges, please.'

She left the greengrocer's shop warily, glancing first one way then another, but there was no sign of Denzil. Instead she walked straight into Helen, looking tanned and radiant.

'Hello, Clare! How are you?' asked Helen, smiling.

'I'm fine,' said Clare huskily, still on edge in case Denzil appeared. Then she took in Helen's appearance and said, 'You look wonderful. Have you just got back from Majorca?'

'Yes, a couple of days ago. Paul and I had to get back to reopen the hotel for the spring season.' A slight flush crept up Helen's brown face. Shyly, she said in a rush, 'We're getting married again, Clare.'

It wasn't exactly a surprise; Paul's concern for her, his insistence that she went away with him to Majorca, had made it plain that he still cared for Helen, but Clare lit up with pleasure.

'That's marvellous, Helen! No wonder you look so happy. When I think what you looked like before Christmas, when you were taken ill—now you're a different woman!'

'That was what brought us together again—my illness. You know, if you hadn't rung him then, Clare, he would have gone off to Majorca alone, and we might never have got together again.'

'I'm sure you would!' Clare protested.

'I don't know about that. We're both stubborn, and far too proud. I owe you, Clare! You will come to the wedding, won't you? It will be quiet, in about a month's time. No fuss, just a quick wedding, and a little party, at the hotel, for family and a few friends.'

'I'd love to. Thank you for inviting me.' Clare took a breath, then, after taking another rapid look

up and down the High Street to check that Denzil
was nowhere around, very casually asked, 'By the
way, is Denzil Black still your client?'

Helen's face changed—she went pink, frowned,
looked down. 'No, Johnny Pritchard took over his
account, don't you remember? Why?'

'He's renting a cottage from us, while Dark Tarn
is being done up. I wondered if you were repre-
senting him again, now you're OK.'

'No.' Helen's voice was curt.

Clare decided to take the risk of being frank with
her. 'Helen, I'm worried about Lucy... I've just
found out that she's been seeing him, secretly.'

Helen looked at her sharply, her eyes wide and
shaken. 'Lucy? But isn't she engaged?'

'Yes, to a very nice guy who's working in Africa
at the moment. She hasn't seen him for nine
months, she's bored and lonely, I'm afraid, and
from the minute she set eyes on Denzil Black she
was fascinated by him.'

Helen bit her lip. 'Then you're right to be worried
about her. He's bad news to women.' Her flush
deepened; she gave Clare a grimace. 'I ought to
know; I lost my head over him. I was so miserable
over Paul when I met him, I didn't think I could
feel worse, but I was wrong. I started seeing Denzil
and I got obsessed with him instead—all I could
think about was him; I was miserable if I didn't see
him, and feverish when I did!'

Clare was pale, disturbed. 'That just about de-
scribes Lucy recently. I thought she was working
too hard. She's stopped talking, except when she
flies into a rage over something unimportant, she

hardly eats a thing, and she's in a daze all the time and looks like a ghost.'

Helen frowned. 'Poor Lucy. I'm sorry for her; I know how she feels because I've been there. God, I felt such a fool once I got over him. I don't know how I came to get into such a state over the man.'

'I think you were right about being vulnerable because of Paul,' Clare said sympathetically, and Helen nodded.

'Yes. I met Denzil, and he was very kind and understanding.' She caught Clare's cynical expression and stopped, said insistently, 'No, he really was! He was supportive, very sympathetic, and I was looking for something, anything, to stop me fretting for Paul, so I got hooked on Denzil Black instead. Transference, they call it. You transfer the way you feel for one man to the guy who's trying to help you get over it.' She laughed edgily. 'It doesn't help, either. In a way, it was worse—I stopped eating, didn't sleep, couldn't think of anything else, but it was all so unreal, the way I felt. It was a sort of nervous breakdown, I suppose. No wonder I collapsed in the end. Once I was back with Paul I realised that that whole affair with Denzil had been pure moonshine. I was never in love with him and he was simply amusing himself with me.' Her voice grew wry, so did her face. 'He's a very sophisticated guy, plays games with people, especially women.'

Clare listened tensely, watching her with a mixture of pity, impatience and dismay.

Soberly, Helen added, 'Lucy's much too young to know how to handle him, Clare. She could get badly hurt if she takes his games too seriously.'

'I know,' said Clare slowly. 'That's what's scaring me. I can't think how to put a stop to it. He wouldn't listen to me, and neither would Lucy.'

'Can't you persuade Mike to come home earlier? Bring the marriage forward?'

'That's an idea.' Clare's eyes lit up. 'I'm sure Lucy still loves him.'

Helen smiled at her. 'Well, I hope it works out for her. I like Lucy. Sorry, I must rush, I've got a lot to do today. I'll send you a wedding invitation when they're ready. See you, Clare.'

That evening over dinner, Clare casually asked Lucy, 'When is Mike coming home, exactly? Shouldn't we be starting to make arrangements for the wedding soon?'

Lucy's face was snow-white. 'Mike isn't coming home,' she said without looking up.

Everyone sat up, looked sharply at her.

'Not coming home?' repeated Clare, taken aback and incredulous. 'What do you mean?'

'He's been offered a three-year contract out there, and he wants to accept it. He isn't planning to come home again until the contract is over.' Lucy's voice was high, shrill, quivering. Her pale lips trembled as she spoke.

'But what's happening about the wedding? Is it postponed or——?'

'He actually asked me to fly to Africa and get married out there!' Lucy burst out angrily. 'None of my friends could come, even if you managed to afford the fare there and back! It wouldn't be a real wedding; I always planned to get married in our own church, with bridesmaids, and flowers, and the organ playing and...' She got up, pushing back her chair, a sob in her throat. 'Well, I'm not settling for some quick ceremony in a strange place, with nobody much there, so he can forget it!'

She ran out of the room and Robin let out a long whistle, his face rueful. 'Boy, is she going to be a little ray of sunshine in the house after this! Why couldn't Mike just come home and marry her, and then tell her about Africa?'

Clare and her father exchanged looks.

'Now we know why she's been so odd lately, Clare!'

'Have you got Mike's address in Africa, Dad? They must have a phone at this training college, surely? Maybe if we talked to him we could persuade him to come home to get married?'

'Maybe we could, but even if he did I wonder if Lucy would really want to live in Africa afterwards?'

Her father's gentle voice made Clare frown. 'I can understand her feeling cheated because she won't be getting the sort of wedding she has always dreamed about, Dad! Lucy's always been a romantic girl. I don't think she meant that she wouldn't want to live in Africa, just that she wanted her dream wedding first.'

'I wonder,' said George Summer drily. 'I suspect Lucy is reacting against any change of any sort. She's never lived anywhere else, and she doesn't want to; she's still rather childish, I'm afraid. Or else, if this is what Mike has chosen to do with his life, and she loves him, wouldn't she accept his decision without throwing a tantrum and sulking about it?' He shook his head, sighing. 'No, I don't think we should intervene, Clare. This is between the two of them. Mike has obviously found a place he likes, and wants to live in, and a job he loves doing. Lucy has to face that. If you want to talk to anyone, talk to Lucy—get her to see that life isn't a simple matter of other people doing what she wants, giving in to her all the time. Marriage, in particular, means compromising, two people working things out between them on a share and share alike basis, fifty-fifty. Frankly, I don't think Lucy has grown up enough for that.'

Clare said wryly, 'Maybe it's our fault; maybe we spoiled her.'

'No maybe about it,' said Robin, laughing. 'Lucy's sweet, but she is used to getting her own way, you can't deny that. I did wonder how she would cope with married life. Mike's no pushover, you know. He wouldn't let her run rings around him the way she does around you and Dad.'

Laughing, Clare made faces at him, but in her heart she knew there was some truth in what he and her father had just said. Lucy had been spoilt, but that didn't stop Clare worrying about what was happening between her and Denzil Black. Even more now, in fact; it was clear that Lucy was very vulnerable at the moment. That was how Denzil Black had been able to move in on her.

The question was, how seriously was Lucy involved with him? Was he just helping her over a bad time, or was there more to it than that?

She was clearing the dinner-table later when she heard Lucy's footsteps in the hall, making for the front door. Clare hurried out to intercept her.

'I'm going out!' Lucy defiantly told her, eyes suspiciously pink around the rims.

'At this hour? It's nearly nine!'

'I'm not a child! Stop treating me like one!'

Clare felt like slapping her like a naughty child, but kept her temper with an effort.

Perhaps reading her expression, Lucy added hurriedly, 'As it happens, I've got to see someone about the school pageant.'

'Denzil Black?' asked Clare acidly, and saw the flicker of startled apprehension in Lucy's eyes.

'What?' Lucy was playing for time, trying to guess how much Clare knew, and how much she was guessing, and trying to work out what to say to placate her.

'I know you've been seeing him, and he's been helping with the pageant, Lucy,' Clare said in cool tones. 'Your headmistress told me all about it. Why didn't you mention it to me? You never even told me you'd seen him again.'

Lucy's mouth turned down at the edges. 'I knew how you'd react. You'd made it clear you didn't want me seeing him; I didn't want a long argument with you about it.'

'I never thought you'd be so secretive,' Clare reproached her. 'How long has this been going on?'

Sulkily, Lucy said, 'I ran into him one weekend, in town, and told him about the pageant, and when I just happened to say I could do with some advice on how to stage it he was really nice and offered to come along and see if he could help.'

'You just happened to drop a damned great hint,' said Clare drily.

Lucy gave her a furious look. 'All right, maybe I was obvious, but it was an opportunity I couldn't miss. Everyone at school was thrilled, and I think Denzil's had a wonderful time, too. He's really interested; he's come up with all sorts of great ideas for us. He treated it like a real professional job, not just an amateur school effort.'

'I doubt if someone like him would do something he saw as an amateur effort,' Clare said, frowning. 'The man is an important professional; you had no right to ask him to do this . . .'

'Well, he could easily have said he was too busy!' snapped Lucy. 'But he didn't. I think he's been enjoying himself. I know the kids adore him.' She glared at Clare. 'And so do I! OK? That's what you want to know, isn't it? You suspect I'm falling for him. You're pretty obvious. What's been going on? That's what you're dying to ask. I know what you think. Well, he hasn't been trying to seduce me, he has just been very sweet and thoughtful and kind.'

'I can imagine!' said Clare, her eyes dark blue with rage.

'No, you can't! You haven't got any imagination. You've just got a nasty mind. I needed someone to talk to, I told him my problems, and

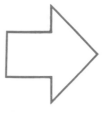

# NO COST! NO OBLIGATION TO BUY!
# NO PURCHASE NECESSARY!

## PLAY "LUCKY 7" AND GET FIVE FREE GIFTS!

# HOW TO PLAY:

1. With a coin, carefully scratch off the silver box at the right. Then check the claim chart to see what we have for you—FREE BOOKS and a gift—ALL YOURS! ALL FREE!

2. Send back this card and you'll receive brand-new Harlequin Presents® novels. These books have a cover price of $3.25 each, but they are yours to keep absolutely free.

3. There's no catch. You're under no obligation to buy anything. We charge nothing—ZERO—for your first shipment. And you don't have to make any minimum number of purchases—not even one!

4. The fact is thousands of readers enjoy receiving books by mail from the Harlequin Reader Service®. They like the convenience of home delivery . . . they like getting the best new novels months before they're available in stores . . . and they love our discount prices!

5. We hope that after receiving your free books you'll want to remain a subscriber. But the choice is yours—to continue or cancel, anytime at all! So why not take us up on our invitation, with no risk of any kind. You'll be glad you did!

You'll love this plush, cuddly Teddy Bear, an adorable accessory for your dressing table, bookcase or desk. Measuring 5½" tall, he's soft and brown and has a bright red ribbon around his neck—he's completely captivating! And he's yours *absolutely free*, when you accept this no-risk offer!

# PLAY "LUCKY 7"

**Just scratch off the silver box with a coin.**
**Then check below to see the gifts you get.**

**YES!** I have scratched off the silver box. Please send me all the gifts for which I qualify. I understand I am under no obligation to purchase any books, as explained on the back and on the opposite page.

106 CIH ASYL
(U-H-P-02/95)

NAME

ADDRESS                                                    APT.

CITY                              STATE              ZIP

left margin
**DETACH AND MAIL CARD TODAY**

| | | | |
|---|---|---|---|
|  | | | **WORTH FOUR FREE BOOKS PLUS A FREE CUDDLY TEDDY BEAR** |
| | | | **WORTH THREE FREE BOOKS** |
|  | | | **WORTH TWO FREE BOOKS** |
|  | | | **WORTH ONE FREE BOOK** |

Offer limited to one per household and not valid to current Harlequin Presents® subscribers. All orders subject to approval.

© 1990 HARLEQUIN ENTERPRISES LIMITED          **PRINTED IN U.S.A.**

## THE HARLEQUIN READER SERVICE®: HERE'S HOW IT WORKS

Accepting free books places you under no obligation to buy anything. You may keep the books and gift and return the shipping statement marked "cancel". If you do not cancel, about a month later we'll send you 6 additional novels, and bill you just $2.44 each plus 25¢ delivery and applicable sales tax, if any.* That's the complete price, and—compared to cover prices of $3.25 each—quite a bargain! You may cancel at any time, but if you choose to continue, every month we'll send you 6 more books, which you may either purchase at the discount price...or return at our expense and cancel your subscription.

*Terms and prices subject to change without notice. Sales tax applicable in N.Y.

If offer card is missing, write to: Harlequin Reader Service, 3010 Walden Ave., P.O. Box 1867, Buffalo, NY 14269-1867

## BUSINESS REPLY MAIL
FIRST CLASS MAIL   PERMIT NO. 717   BUFFALO, NY

POSTAGE WILL BE PAID BY ADDRESSEE

HARLEQUIN READER SERVICE
3010 WALDEN AVE
PO BOX 1867
BUFFALO NY 14240-9952

NO POSTAGE
NECESSARY
IF MAILED
IN THE
UNITED STATES

he listened. That was all I needed; just a shoulder to cry on, someone who seemed to care about me, took me seriously.'

Angrily, Clare said, 'It wasn't him you should have been talking to, it was Mike!'

'What's the point of talking to Mike when he's made up his mind what he wants out of life and hasn't even bothered to ask what sort of life I want? We obviously don't have a thing in common any more.'

Clare was appalled and gave her a stricken look. Things were far worse than she had thought.

'Lucy, you love Mike—you've been engaged for months. You could at least talk this out with him; you can't just walk away. Doesn't he deserve that? How can he know what you feel if you don't talk to him?'

'If Denzil could listen, why can't Mike?'

'Denzil Black isn't doing you any favours by encouraging you to talk to him instead of the man you're supposed to be marrying. Lucy, he's bad for you; stop seeing so much of him. You're beginning to look the way Helen did before she collapsed with anaemia.'

'I haven't got anaemia!' Lucy laughed furiously. 'Don't drag Helen into this! Denzil didn't make her ill—Helen was always a bit of a neurotic.'

'That's not true! Helen was always lively and cheerful until she met Denzil Black.'

Lucy hesitated, then said crossly, 'Well, anyway, what has any of that to do with me? She's back with Paul now and the last time I saw her she looked fine.'

Clare sighed, unable to deny that Helen was now safely over Denzil, but she wasn't giving up. 'Lucy, why don't you ring Mike and talk frankly to him? I'll pay for the call. Ring him now, tonight.'

Lucy's skin was utterly bloodless, her mouth quivered. 'No, I don't want to talk to him. It's over. I'm sending him his ring back. Look, I've got to go. I told Denzil I'd be there by nine, and I'm late now.'

'Why is it so urgent to see him about the pageant tonight?' Clare asked impatiently and Lucy looked at her with glittering, wild eyes.

'OK, it isn't about the pageant—I just have to see him.'

An icy hand clutched at Clare's heart. 'Lucy, don't go,' she pleaded, trying to put an arm around her. 'He's dangerous to you, can't you see that? Look at yourself, for heaven's sake—you look terrible!'

Lucy flung her off. 'Denzil doesn't think so! He says I'm very photogenic. So there! He wants to give me a film test. He's going to put me in his new film!'

# CHAPTER FIVE

CLARE had a bad night. How could she sleep when her sister was hell bent on ruining her life?

'You don't actually think he's serious!' Clare had made the mistake of saying angrily when Lucy told her about this talk of a film test and a part in Denzil Black's new film.

'Lots of people have told me I should be in films!' Lucy had retorted, taking a sidelong look into a mirror on the wall near by, admiring her own reflection. Clare had compounded her mistaken approach first by laughing at her sister's childlike vanity, and then by teasing her.

'Lots of men wanting to date you, you mean, don't you?'

She had got a furious look, of course. Pink and spluttering, Lucy had snapped back, 'Denzil means what he says—he isn't just shooting me a line! I'm going to have the film test on Saturday, so there!'

Clare had been silenced, her face stunned. Lucy had given her a triumphant little smile, satisfied by her sister's reaction.

'And don't think you can stop me going,' she had then added fiercely. 'It's my life, not yours. I'm not a child any more, so stop trying to interfere!'

How could Clare do that? Ever since their mother's death Clare had been responsible for Lucy and the two boys. George Summer was a loving father but he was conventional in his thinking—he had been brought up to believe that it was a woman's job to bring up children and run the home, so when his wife was no longer there to do it he had left her role to her eldest daughter without thinking twice about it, and Clare had never tried to wriggle out of doing what she, too, saw as her duty. The younger children at that time had all needed to be mothered, watched over, cared for— it hadn't always been easy but Clare had done her best.

Her own life would have been very different if she had been free to do as she liked, have fun, go out every night, live for herself.

Over the years new relationships had withered and died because she had so little free time. Men expected you to have time for them. They didn't want to wait in line for your attention, competing with a little boy with measles or a father in bed with flu who needed constant nursing. Even the most patient men gave up and walked away in the end.

She hadn't been serious about any of them, of course, except Hal, and, looking back at that affair now, she realised that she had never given Hal all her attention, either, so maybe he wasn't entirely to blame for the way he had behaved. She had always been too absorbed in caring for the family to commit herself, really fall in love. Maybe it had become a habit and maybe Lucy was right—she was still trying to run her sister's life for her. But when she saw Lucy walking straight into danger, how could she stand back and let her do it?

She spent the night worrying, got up dark-eyed and pale, and had no appetite for breakfast. Looking at herself in the mirror, she ruefully recognised that she was beginning to look like one of Denzil Black's victims.

A shiver ran through her.

What on earth had made her think that? It would never happen to her. Never. She saw him too clearly. A man like Denzil Black could never operate by daylight; he needed moonlight and romantic music as his allies, and he always went for women like Helen and Lucy, who were unhappy, lonely, yearning for a little romance.

Well, he wasn't getting away with it. Not with Lucy. Fiercely, Clare decided that she was going to rescue her sister, even if Lucy didn't want to be rescued. It might be for the last time, but Clare wasn't going to stand aside and watch her sister ruining her life, when there was something she could do to stop it.

She began that morning by ringing Mike at the training college where he was teaching.

He had a grim note in his voice. 'Are you ringing me to tell me Lucy has met someone else?'

Clare was taken aback. 'What makes you think——?' she began, and he interrupted,

'I'm not stupid. I can read between the lines in her letters. She's changed over the last few months.'

'Mike, she's very upset about you, not over someone else. She had looked forward to her wedding-day for such a long time—maybe you don't realise how much that sort of thing matters to a woman.' Clare talked rapidly, explaining, trying to make him see Lucy's point of view.

When she paused, Mike said impatiently, 'But if I fly home for a few weeks, to get married, and have a honeymoon, it will cost a lot of money. I thought it would be best if we skipped the expensive wedding and my trip home, and used that money to buy things for our new home over here. It seemed the sensible thing to do.'

'Of course, you're right,' soothed Clare gently. 'But Mike . . . Lucy is romantic, she has her heart set on a white wedding, with her family and friends all there, in the church she's known all her life. That's the way she wants to start her life with you— it's the way her mind works, Mike; she sets great store by the family, by traditions. Even when she was a little girl she loved to hear bedtime stories the same way every time. She hates changes to her routine, and she's very conventionally minded.' She paused and softly said, 'Isn't that one of the things you love most about her? Aren't you the same?'

Mike was silent for a little while, then he said soberly, 'You think I should give in to her? Agree to a big white wedding back home?'

'I'm sure Lucy loves you, Mike, and she would be very unhappy if she lost you. Look, I have an idea—I think Lucy ought to make a trip out to visit you at once, see for herself where you'll both be living. Her school has a half-term holiday starting this Friday. She could come out there for a week.'

Mike sounded startled. 'That would be won-derful but . . . the air fare will be expensive, you know, and I haven't that much money.'

'I'll pay; it can be part of my wedding present to you both. I just want to be sure you'll meet her at the airport and look after her.'

'Of course I will! Don't worry about that!' He was beginning to sound excited and Clare smiled.

'And could you book her into a hotel near you?'

'There's a very good one close to the college, where parents stay when they're visiting the students.' Mike paused, sounded uncertain as he asked, 'Clare, have you talked to her about this idea? I mean, she does want to come? I could ring her and——'

'No, don't ring her, Mike. I wanted to talk to you first, and make sure it was feasible, but I'm sure Lucy will be thrilled. I won't talk to her about it until I've managed to make the bookings. I'll surprise her with the tickets later this week. Leave it all to me. I'll ring you again on Friday morning to tell you what arrangements I've managed to make.'

It was easy to book Lucy's flight, but Clare had other arrangements to make before she talked to her sister.

She drove to the next town later that afternoon and spent some time in various shops. What she wanted was not easy to track down, but at last she managed to get everything. On the Friday afternoon she left her new part-time assistant in charge of the office and returned home when she was certain that nobody else would be in the house. Her father was out playing golf with friends, and of course none of the others was ever home during the day during term-time.

Clare had a very practical turn of mind. She had picked up all sorts of useful information from her father and brothers over the years. George Summer had a very well-equipped workshop in the garden. Clare spent several hours out there, then transferred what she had been working on to the boot of her car, just as her father and Lucy both arrived back.

'You're home early!'

Clare grinned at her father's surprise. 'I took the afternoon off, for a change, relaxed for a while, but I did some cooking too—I've got a casserole in the oven, and I'm just about to pop some jacket potatoes in with it. I'll make you a cup of tea; you can take that up with you while you have your bath.'

Happily, her father sat down and began to take off his muddy golfing shoes, his face healthily flushed, talking about golf all the time, with the fascination of the addict who didn't realise nobody wanted to hear what he was saying.

Clare half listened, half thought about what she planned to do that evening. Excitement lay coiled in the pit of her stomach, every now and then stirring, making her nerves flicker. She found it very hard to concentrate on anything else.

Taking his tea with him, George Summer finally went upstairs, and Clare asked Lucy in a carefully casual voice, 'What are you doing tonight? Going out with Denzil Black again?'

'No, Denzil said he had a lot of paperwork to do tonight. He was going to bed early, and he told me to have a quiet evening, too; relax, get a good night's sleep, so that I'll be rested for tomorrow's test,' Lucy said huskily, her face very pale, then burst out, 'All very well for him to say that, but I'm so nervous I can't relax, and as for sleeping...I'm sure I won't close my eyes all night.'

Clare watched her prowling around the kitchen, picking things up and putting them down, looking out of the window at the daffodils which were in full bloom in the garden outside. Spring was here, the days were longer, and there was a restlessness in the air. Clare felt it herself; she could see that Lucy did too.

'Why don't you go to the cinema? Jamie asked me to take him tonight, but I'm not really in the mood.'

Lucy looked tempted, wavered. 'Denzil did say I should rest...'

'Going to the cinema is restful. You'll just be sitting in the dark, watching a film.'

'Denzil might ring to check up on me!'

'I'll tell him you're resting,' Clare said drily and Lucy laughed.

'You've talked me into it!'

Their father and Robin both had engagements that evening, so by seven-thirty Clare was in the house alone. By a quarter to eight she was on her way to her cottage.

When she parked outside she saw Denzil's face appear at the window upstairs. It was dark by then, and there was a faint light in the room behind him giving a halo to his black head; she shivered as she saw his eyes, narrowed and speculative, his mouth curling at the corners in a disturbing smile.

He was wearing a loose black silk shirt—or was it a pyjama top? she wondered as he opened the window to speak to her. The night wind blew his shirt backwards, and she saw beneath the soft material the hard outline of his body: his ribs, his flat stomach, the muscular chest wall. Clare's mouth was dry. She swallowed nervously.

Even from a distance she felt the vibration of his sexuality; deep inside her body she felt her blood beating faster and fear rose up inside her in a tidal wave. Fear for her sister, she told herself. She wasn't afraid for herself; she could deal with him. He didn't frighten her.

'Did you want me?' he asked, and she distinctly heard the taunt under the words and felt her skin burning.

'I want to talk to you,' she said, choosing her words carefully.

'I wondered when I'd hear from you,' he said, mockery glimmering in those dark-pupilled eyes. 'I was sure I would, once you found out that I'd suggested that Lucy have a screen test.'

Clare didn't answer. She was so tense that her teeth grated against each other, making her jaws ache. He was far too shrewd. That bothered her. If he was able to guess her reactions, might he also guess how far she was prepared to go to stop his plans for Lucy?

Pretending coolness, she said, 'Do you think you might come down here? I don't want to have to shout what I have to say.'

'A pity. I was just thinking how romantic this is—the balcony scene from *Romeo and Juliet*, in reverse, with Romeo on the balcony and Juliet standing under his window.'

Clare snapped, 'Will you please come downstairs?'

He laughed. 'You've got no sense of humour; I've noticed that before. OK, but I was reading in bed, and I'm in my pyjamas. I'll just slip on a dressing-gown and be down. Have you still got a key? Let yourself in.'

He shut the window before Clare started replying. 'Get dressed . . .'

Her words died away. She had to pull herself together hurriedly to start putting her plan into operation. She needed a cool head tonight; she must not let him get under her skin. That could be disastrous.

As she let herself into the cottage Denzil was coming down the stairs. He looked magnificent in a black satin quilted dressing-gown over the black pyjamas; Clare felt her breath catch in her throat and was appalled by her unwanted reactions to him.

'Can I get you a drink?' he asked, his grey gaze wandering over her from head to toe, making her feel as if they left fingerprints on her skin.

She was wearing a pale blue angora sweater, a string of pearls around her throat, a pale grey pleated skirt, and over that a short grey jacket which she hadn't bothered to button up because it was

quite a warm night for early spring, and she would
be in the car, anyway. Her clothes, as always, were
classic, simple, very English. The way he stared,
though, made her feel she was half naked, and she
quivered with resentment.

'No, thank you,' she muttered hoping he could
read her hostility in her eyes.

If he did, it merely amused him. He gave her a
mocking smile. 'Well, I do. You look as if you've
come here to make trouble, and if you're going to
be difficult I shall need a stiff drink to help me
cope with you!'

He walked past her towards the kitchen and she
backed against the wall to get out of his way. He
stopped to look down at her, his eyes a flash of fire
that made Clare wince away even further.

'Don't do that!' he bit out.

'What?' she asked defensively and saw his mouth
twist.

'Shrink every time I come within ten feet of you!
What are you afraid I might do?' He moved closer
until he almost touched her and Clare felt her blood
beating in her neck.

'Maybe what you're doing now!' she snapped,
her head lifted, her blue eyes defying him. 'Lay one
finger on me and——'

Smiling lazily, he put out a long index finger and
touched her neck where the hot pulse beat.

'And what?' he whispered.

Clare swallowed, too busy fighting breath-
lessness to be able to speak. He ran the finger slowly
up her throat, following the blue line of her vein.
The beating of her blood grew faster, hotter.

'Stop it!' Clare managed to get out.

His finger leapt to her mouth, caressed the parted, quivering curve of it; she felt as if her lips clung to his skin, and was even more shaken.

'Your mouth is a give-away, you know,' he murmured softly. 'Those blue eyes of yours are cold and say "Hands off, Mister!" but that mouth is pure temptation and says something very different.'

'It says if you don't stop touching me I swear I'll hit you with the nearest blunt instrument!' Clare reached for her anger, to hide the sensual turmoil inside her, and she backed it up by pushing him away with both hands.

Touching him was a mistake. A big mistake. First, because she might as well have tried to push over a solid stone wall. Second, because as her palms flattened against the black satin dressing-gown he moved even closer, trapping her hands between them and making her virtually a prisoner.

Breathless, Clare tried to pull herself free while he watched, his eyes glimmering between half-lowered lids. He was leaning on her quite deliberately, his hands on either side of her head, his body touching hers intimately, from shoulder to thigh.

'Get away from me!' she snarled. 'If you think you can play the sort of games with me that you usually play with women you're wrong!'

'This isn't a game, Clare,' he murmured. 'This is war, and you're my prisoner.' He moved even closer, lowering his voice. 'Poor Clare, a helpless prisoner.' He was smiling with his mouth, but his eyes were deep and dark; they held hers and she couldn't break free.

She had a terrifying urge to close her eyes. His gaze was hypnotic; staring back at him made her head cloud so that thinking was difficult. A languid heaviness crept over her. She didn't want to go on resisting him, fighting how he made her feel—she wanted to let herself go with the hot tide flowing inside her veins. His dark-pupilled eyes probed deep inside her; she looked into them and trembled, aware of his mouth coming down closer, wanting it . . . needing it.

Her head fought with her body, coldly reminding her that this was what he did to women! This feeling taking her over—the weakness, the fever, the need, she recognised it, didn't she? Helen had told her how it felt to be physically obsessed with this man. 'He's bad news to women', Helen had said, and she was right. Clare knew at that instant just how dangerous he could be, and her heart beat heavily inside her.

She would never have been able to stop him kissing her, but as his mouth was about to hit hers the phone began to ring. Denzil stiffened, his head lifting to listen.

'Damn it. Amazing timing some people have. I should have put the answering machine on!'

The ringing went on relentlessly.

He straightened, sighing. 'I'm afraid I'll have to answer it; I'm expecting an important call.' He looked at her under his lashes, smiling. 'Don't go away.'

As he walked away from her into the sitting-room, Clare leaned on the wall, shuddering, dry-mouthed, barely able to stand up.

The ringing stopped and she heard his voice clearly, impatient, curt. 'Yes? Yes, hi, Joe. So, did they go for it?' A pause then he laughed wryly. 'I didn't expect they would...so what's the next move?'

Clare stiffly walked a few steps, but her legs were so weak she had to sit down on the bottom step of the stairs. She listened blankly to the autocratic snap of Denzil's voice in the sitting-room. He couldn't be an easy man to work for, but then he wasn't an easy man in any sense.

Denzil hung up a moment later and came back. By then, she had almost fought her way back to feeling normal again, and was able to confront him without too many nerves.

'Have you told Lucy she could be the new Garbo or something?'

He gave her a dry glance. 'Hardly. I'm not even sure she can act.'

'Then why are you giving her a film test?'

'She's dying to work on a film set, and the camera likes her. I've taken some photos of her; I could see she would look good on film too. My next film is going to be filmed near here...'

'This Brontë film?'

He gave her a crooked smile. 'The local grapevine at work again? Yes, the Brontë film. I shall need lots of extras and there'll be some tiny non-speaking parts.'

Clare was trembling with anger. 'And that's what you're planning for Lucy? That's what she would chuck her marriage over for? A tiny non-speaking role in your next film if she's lucky, and, if not, a few days as an extra in a crowd?'

'Will you stop blaming me for everything that happens to other people? Lucy's problems with her fiancé are nothing to do with me, any more than Helen's illness was anything to do with me.'

Clare's eyes hated him and she saw him frown.

'I'm not even going to waste my time arguing with you,' she told him scornfully. 'But I'm not going to let you ruin my sister's life.' She knew now what she had come here to find out. She stood up. 'I came to collect some things from the locked cabinet in the little bedroom. It shouldn't take me long to find them and then I'll be on my way home.'

She went up the stairs, leaving him standing at the foot of them, staring after her. In the small front bedroom she unlocked the cabinet, which was the only piece of furniture in the room and which held most of her documents to do with the house. She lifted them out, then went out of the room again, on tiptoe, and listened. She could hear Denzil moving about in the kitchen. Softly she went into the bedroom he was using and set to work in there. After a few minutes she crept out again and went back to the small room and began leafing through the documents.

A short time later, she heard Denzil coming up the stairs. He came towards the open door, stood there, watching her.

Clare looked over her shoulder. 'I've almost finished here.'

'I brought you a drink,' he said, putting a glass down on top of the cabinet.

Clare frowned at the colourless contents. 'Is that gin?'

'Yes, gin and tonic.'

'I'm sorry, I don't really like gin. I don't suppose you have any orange juice?'

'Of course—what do you want with it?'

'Nothing, just the juice would be fine.'

He shrugged, put his own glass down and went back downstairs. Clare opened her bag and got out two little pills; she palmed them just as she heard Denzil coming back, his footsteps fast and light on the stairs.

He offered her the glass of orange juice. She took it. 'Thank you.' She drank a little and Denzil turned to pick up his own glass.

Keeping a wary eye on his back, Clare dropped the pills into her glass, whirled the glass rapidly until they dissolved. She put the glass to her lips as Denzil turned to face her, then frowned obviously, lowering the glass again, staring down into it.

'Did you put gin in this?'

His brows met. 'No, you said you didn't like it.'

'Well, it tastes odd.'

'What do you mean, odd?'

She held out the glass. 'Taste it yourself.'

His eyes angry, he took the glass, lifted it to his mouth, drank some of the juice. 'There's no gin in this—or anything else. It does have a faintly acid taste, but then orange juice sometimes does.'

She wanted to be sure he had drunk enough. Her voice cold, she asked, 'Did you actually drink any of it, or just take a tiny sip?'

He gave her a level, unsmiling stare, took another long swallow from the glass, grated, 'You see? Nothing wrong with it. But don't drink it if you aren't happy about it.'

He put the glass down on top of the cabinet with a little crash, and Clare jumped, her already tense nerves reverberating.

'There's no need to lose your temper! I thought it tasted strange, that's all.'

His eyes were angry, his mouth a straight, cold line. 'What did you think I'd done to your drink, spiked it to get you drunk? And then what? Rape? Is that what you thought I had in mind?'

Her hands shaking slightly, she locked the cabinet, not looking at him. 'Look, I'm sorry, OK?' she muttered.

'No, it isn't OK,' Denzil bit out. 'I've never needed to make a woman drunk before I could get her into bed.'

Clare lost her temper too. 'Oh, haven't you? Well, you'd have to knock me down with a brick!'

'If I had a brick handy right now I'd be tempted to use it!' he threw back. 'But not to get you into bed, believe me! I'm not that desperate for a woman!'

Her face burned. She turned on her heel, walked furiously, unsteadily, out of the room. He followed close behind her, almost cannoning into her when she stopped outside the open door of his bedroom, remembering just in time that she was in the process of ruining her own plans by losing her temper.

She pulled herself together, tried to look a little more friendly. 'I see you've made yourself comfortable,' she murmured, looking into the softly lamplit room. She had vaguely noticed the changes earlier, when she was in here, but she hadn't had time then to look closely at anything. Now she did, thinking that it was nothing like the room she remembered, that cell-like white-painted room which had so little furniture. The walls were now a warm apricot shade; new curtains in a deeper shade hung at the windows. He had put in a number of lamps, a desk by the window, a deep leather armchair with a small table beside it, some bookcases. The walls were thick with paintings, watercolours, sketches, prints.

He gave a sudden yawn, looked surprised, and said sleepily, 'You don't object to the changes I've made?'

She lowered her lashes, looked sideways at him, saw him yawn again. 'Of course not; you've made it into a very warm room. I love the apricot walls. Must be wonderful first thing in the morning when the sun comes up. And what a lot of pictures—do you paint?'

'Some of the watercolours and sketches are mine,' he casually agreed.

'Really? Which ones?' She walked into the room and looked at one of the sketches and Denzil came up behind her, yawning convulsively.

'Yes, that's one of mine.'

'It's very good,' she said, quite surprised by just how good. He could really draw; the sketch of a landscape had very few details, but the black lines had force and impact, caught the eye.

'I do my own story-boards,' he shrugged. 'That's a sketch for a background we used in a film of mine. I need to visualise every detail before I start shooting, plan every frame so that we know what we're going to need. Look, here's an interior, a scene in a house, from my last film.'

She looked at the framed sketch and had a vague memory of the scene in the film, a particularly intense and sexy scene where the Irish-Mexican actress had danced, naked, for her lover. It was odd, seeing this first visualisation of it, even the people sketched in with light, flowing lines, their faces mere ovals without expression, and yet the erotic nature of the scene unmistakable.

He yawned again and she gave him a quick, sideways look. 'Sorry about this,' he said, frowning. 'I told you I was tired, but I didn't realise I was this tired.' He staggered backwards and sat down on the bed suddenly, looking puzzled.

Clare went over and put a hand to his forehead. 'Maybe you've got this flu that's been going around. It's a pretty violent bug, but it only lasts twenty-four hours. You'd better lie down.'

'I can't, I must see you downstairs and——' He broke off. 'God, I feel weird.'

Clare gently pushed him backwards. He gave no resistance, simply collapsed slowly on to the bed like a rag doll, his eyes closing.

'My head . . .' he mumbled, and then there was silence except for the soft drag of his breathing, his mouth open, his face flushed.

Clare bent over him, listened, watching him intently. He was completely out. She was torn between amazement and triumph. Her plan had worked, without any difficulty at all! She had been afraid the sleeping pills would take far longer to affect him so she had doubled the dose recommended by the doctor, and it had certainly hit him fast.

She took a deep breath. She couldn't afford to waste time congratulating herself; she had things to do before he came to—she had no real idea how long that would take. He could wake up in five minutes or in five hours, Clare wasn't sure which. She had been to the doctor for the sleeping pills, making up some story about being so overworked that she couldn't sleep and was getting more and more tired. Her doctor had warned her that she might wake up again during the night, but if she did she wasn't to take another pill as they were very strong and could have serious side-effects.

Clare had pretended to be alarmed and asked, 'If I did forget, and take another pill, would it be dangerous?'

'Well, the point is, you could double the dose without harmful effects once, but not habitually,' he had told her. 'The trouble is, people start taking these pills for granted; they wake up at night and forget how many they've taken, so take another one! It would be safer not to keep the pills beside your bed. Put them back in your medicine cabinet once you've taken your night's dose, to be on the safe side.'

Clare frowned, looking at Denzil's sleeping face. She didn't want to do him any harm, even if he was an emotional vampire who threatened her sister's happiness.

She listened to his regular breathing. It seemed normal.

She set to work, stripping off the magnificent black satin dressing-gown because its sleeves were so thickly quilted that they made it hard for her to fix handcuffs on Denzil's wrists.

His dead weight wasn't easy to handle. She had to kneel on the bed beside him, hauling him up with one arm under him, then propping him up against her knee while she got the dressing-gown off, slid the handcuffs around his wrists, clicked them shut. She had earlier fitted them on to the bottom rail of the bedhead, carefully hiding their presence behind one of the banked-up pillows.

Denzil certainly liked to live comfortably; his bedlinen was expensive and perfectly matched the new décor of the room.

As she lowered him again she saw that in her struggle with him somehow his pyjama-top had unbuttoned. Between the lapels she saw the sheen of his smooth brown shoulders, the rough darkness of hair growing down his bare chest.

Her mouth dry, Clare looked away. She didn't want to be made aware of him that way. Angrily, she reached over to do up the jacket, but at that instant Denzil stirred, making a groaning sound, as if about to wake up.

Clare jumped, retreated from the bed, listened, watching him. He moved slightly, tried to turn over, couldn't because his arms were handcuffed back above his head.

A little frown creased his forehead. Clare held
her breath. Sighing, Denzil lay still again.

Clare went back to the bed, took off his leather
slippers, leaving his feet bare. He had quite large
feet, but elegantly shaped, she noted; long and thin
with gracefully shaped toes, a dusting of black hair
on the upper skin.

Clare groaned. Keep your mind on what you're
doing! she scolded herself. And stop looking at him!

She hurriedly got the washing-line out of her bag
and tied his feet together. Handcuffed to the bed,
he couldn't actually get up, but it would be safer
to immobilise him altogether.

There was a telephone right next to his bed. Clare
unplugged it and moved it out of his reach, but left
it in the room because it was an essential part of
her plan that he should ring Lucy when he woke
up.

She set to work again after that with a screw-
driver and a second set of handcuffs attached to a
long, very strong chain. After she had finished, and
checked on Denzil, finding him still heavily asleep,
she quietly went downstairs and made herself some
strong coffee, then went back upstairs to wait.

She looked along his bookcase, found a copy of
Sherlock Holmes stories, and tried to read, but it
was hard to keep her attention on Dr Watson's nar-
rative. Her eyes kept wandering from the page to
the half-naked body of the man sprawled on the
bed.

Every breath he took made his bare chest rise
and fall. The room was warm but she suddenly
realised he could be cold; the body temperature did

fluctuate during sleep. She went over to the bed to pull the quilt up over him.

As she bent down his lids flickered and she froze, watching a silvery gleam show between his lashes for a moment or so before his lids lay still again.

Maybe he had been dreaming? That characteristic flicker of the lids suggested REM sleep—the rapid eye movement which usually meant that someone was dreaming. What had he been dreaming about? she wondered, watching the way his thick black lashes lay against his flushed cheek.

Did he have a temperature? Anxiety quickened in her. She brushed a hand gently against his cheekbones; his skin was warm but not overhot.

She should have gone back to her book then, but the temptation of looking at him while he was unaware of her was too strong. She sat down on the edge of the bed, slowly reached out to brush her fingers over the rough hairs on his bare chest; they prickled against her skin, sending a slow shiver through her.

She tried to think rationally. He was really quite thin; his arms stretched above his head seemed to elongate his body. She remembered the way his shadow had elongated in her dream on Christmas Eve—and closed her eyes, sighing at the memory. She could count his ribs. She slowly touched each one, like a blind woman feeling her way over him, slid her fingertips up his collarbone to his shoulder, to his neck, felt her way up to his face. His jawline was stubbled, a dark shadow on his skin, his firm, cool lips apart as he breathed through them. She touched them and shivered, feeling the strength and sexual promise of their curve.

A piercing excitement made her mouth dry. She nervously licked her lips, swallowing, very flushed, breathing audibly.

She was dying to kiss him. Her stomach was clenched in a feeling that horrified her.

She stared fixedly at him, trembling. He was out of it. He'd never know. She could do what she liked, and he wouldn't know anything about it.

His head turned on the pillow at that instant; she looked at his long, powerful throat, the muscled power relaxed in sleep, and remembered again that dream on Christmas Eve, his mouth at her own throat, her sense of weakness and helplessness.

Now he was helpless, weak, at her mercy. She bent fiercely and buried her mouth in his neck, groaning with wild pleasure at the taste and smell of his skin, picking up the beat of his blood in the blue vein buried inside that skin. Oh, but this was stupid, she thought, it was crazy. What on earth did she think she was doing? If he came to and caught her kissing him what on earth would he think?

She hurriedly sat up again and as she did so a pearl brooch she was wearing on her sweater was dislodged, the pin open, its sharp point scratching his bare chest, drawing a tiny bead of blood.

Clare closed the brooch pin again, staring at the red drop on his skin. It was only a surface scratch but the sight of his blood fascinated her. She closed her eyes and bent her head again, her tongue

moving slowly on his skin, in dream-like
absorption.

After a minute she sat up, very flushed, pulled
the quilt over him, and made herself go back to
her chair, forced herself to concentrate on her book.
She fell asleep herself after a while, in spite of the
strong coffee, her head dropping sideways against
the leather arm of the chair. The book fell to the
floor without disturbing her.

What did wake her was a sound from the man
on the bed. A groan, a movement, then a grunt of
surprise.

Disorientated, Clare woke up, couldn't remember where she was for a second, or what was
happening, then she did remember and flashed a
look towards the bed.

Denzil's eyes were open. Wide open. He was
struggling to get up, dragging on the handcuffs, his
feet, tied together, kicking helplessly.

'What the hell is all this?'

# CHAPTER SIX

CLARE got up and Denzil's head turned sharply. She saw the surprise in his grey eyes as they widened then narrowed again to a hard point of light.

'I'm sorry,' she said, hot colour sweeping up her face under that stare.

'Did you do this to me?' He sounded incredulous and she could understand why he would. 'How the hell . . . what did you hit me with?'

'I put sleeping pills in your drink.'

'You did what?' He stared fixedly at her, scowling. 'If this is your idea of a joke, I don't find it very funny.' He tugged at his imprisoned wrists again. 'Get these damned things off me!'

She came closer to the bed, secure in the knowledge that he couldn't get at her, and began explaining, her voice fast and husky.

'I'm sorry I had to do it this way, but I couldn't think of anything else. I had to stop you, I can't let you ruin my sister's life. I'm getting Lucy away tomorrow, to join her fiancé in Africa. If she has a film test and gets some small part in your next film she'll break off her engagement to Mike and I know that would be a disastrous mistake because Lucy loves him and when she came to her senses it would be too late, so I have to stop her doing that film test tomorrow and the only way I could think of stopping it was to stop you taking her, and I

123

knew you wouldn't listen to reason if I tried to talk you out of it, so——'

As she broke off, too breathless to finish that sentence, Denzil said through clenched teeth, 'My God, you're completely crazy!' and began struggling again, yanking on his handcuffs, trying to break the washing-line holding his feet together.

'You're just wasting your time and energy!' Clare told him, and he turned to glare at her, his lips curled back in wolf-like rage.

'Get me out of this, damn you!'

She shook her head stubbornly. 'No, and if you keep struggling with the cuffs like that you'll hurt yourself.'

He breathed as if he was about to explode.

'Unlock them, then!'

Her nerves jumped at the raw scrape of his voice. Even tied up and helpless like that, he was terrifying, but she mustn't let him see he could frighten her. She struggled to keep her face calm.

He lay there, breathing roughly, visibly thinking, watching her, and then he tried a different approach. He gave her a slow smile, his face, his voice changing, soft and reasonable, full of coaxing charm.

'OK, you win, Clare. No film test for Lucy tomorrow. I give you my word. All right? Now undo these handcuffs.'

She shook her head and saw the sweet reason dissolve from his face, saw the leap of violence in his eyes.

'When I do get out of this you're going to wish you'd never been born!'

She swallowed. She believed him, but she couldn't think about that now. She would have to worry about that later. She had no doubt she would.

'I want you to talk to Lucy,' she said flatly and Denzil lay still again, staring at her, his black brows together.

'Is she here too?' He looked as if he could believe anything now.

'Of course not!' Clare glanced at her watch. It was half-past eleven. Lucy would be back from the cinema, and on her way to bed. There was just time for the call.

She plugged the phone back into the socket and stood facing him, holding the phone in her hand. 'First, you must promise to say exactly what I tell you to say, and nothing else.'

'Why should I?' he enquired, watching her with a worryingly unreadable expression now.

'Because until you've made this call you aren't getting out of those handcuffs.'

'You can't be serious!' he said, and laughed, but his eyes were a million miles from amusement.

'I mean every word,' said Clare. 'Either you agree to make this call or I'm going, and leaving you here, like that, all night.'

His temper flared again. Furiously, he snarled at her, 'This may seem like a joke to you, but it isn't funny! The law won't find it funny, either. Do you know what the penalties are for an offence like this? Technically I'd say you could be charged with assault and forcible detention against my will. You could go to prison for a very long time, and, believe me, you wouldn't like prison life much. It isn't comfortable or pleasant, especially for a girl like you.'

A shiver ran down her spine, but she wasn't backing off; it was too late to worry about what might happen afterwards, when he got free. She had gone too far to call a halt. She was going to see it through.

'I don't think you'll want to tell the police that you were tied up and handcuffed to a bed by a woman,' she said coolly. 'They might laugh.'

His eyes flashed and she saw his teeth come together as if he would like to be biting her head off.

Clare added, shrugging, 'And then there's the publicity once the story got out. Every tabloid would go to town on the story. Pages of it, day after day. I can see the headlines now. They'd love it, but would you? Can you imagine the sort of jokes people would make? Think about it. I might go to prison, but you would be a laughing-stock.'

She saw him thinking. His face was a battle-ground and he looked at her as if he could kill her.

Clare waited a second, then said, 'I'm leaving in five minutes, if you haven't made this call to my sister. So, make up your mind!'

For a moment he lay immobile, watching her, then he said curtly, 'What is it you want me to say to her?'

Relief made her feel almost sick. Once he made that phone call her plans would be safely under way.

'I want you to tell Clare that you're sorry but the film test is off, and you have to go away; you aren't sure when you'll be back.'

'And what stops me making another call as soon as you free me?' he drawled, lifting black brows enquiringly.

'By then Lucy will be on her way to catch her plane.'

She watched him thinking that over.

'You said that once I made the call you would unlock these handcuffs.'

'I will, but I'm not leaving you here alone, and you won't be making any more phone calls.'

A gleam showed in his eyes. 'You intend to stay here with me all night?'

She didn't like the look he gave her; she particularly did not like what she could read in his face but she pretended not to guess what he was thinking.

'Most of it, yes,' she said flatly. 'Well, are you going to make the call or not?'

He gave her a mocking smile. 'OK.'

'Just tell her——' she began, and he interrupted, 'I know what you want me to say.'

'Don't add a word or leave anything out, because if I think you're going to I'll just cut you off!'

He didn't answer, his expression answer enough.

Clare dialled the number, heard the ringing begin, and after a few rings stop, followed by Lucy's voice, rather uncertainly saying, 'Hello?'

Clare held the phone next to Denzil's mouth, ready to snatch it away if he didn't keep to what she wanted him to say.

His voice sounded casual, offhand, she was glad to hear. 'Lucy? Denzil here; sorry to disturb you so late at night, but I have to vanish for a while. I'm afraid the film test is off.'

She heard the buzz of Lucy's voice and could imagine how her sister must be feeling. She bent closer, trying to hear what Lucy was saying, and her pale silky hair fell against Denzil's face. She felt a jab of electricity leap between them and moved away again in a hurry while his grey eyes watched her intently. But he couldn't know that that brief contact had made her heart beat like a hammer against her ribs, sent her pulses racing out of all control...

'I've no idea when I'll be free to see you again, Lucy,' he said into the phone she still held at his mouth. His stare stayed on Clare's face, mockery in his eyes. 'I'm rather tied up at the moment. I'm not my own master.'

Clare fumed at the double meaning. His mouth was crooked with amusement she did not share.

She pulled the phone away and heard Lucy's voice tearfully saying, 'Denzil...but what about the film? Are you still making it? I thought you were sure I was right for that part. Can't you do the test later? Or have you found someone else? Is that it?'

Denzil heard that too. Clare's eyes met his. She did not like the way he looked at her. She mouthed, 'Say goodbye!' and put the mouthpiece closer to him again.

'I'm afraid I'm forced to say goodbye now, Lucy,' Denzil said quite gently. 'I'm sorry.'

Clare hung up and straightened, sighing. She unplugged the phone from the wall again.

'I have to go home now, and talk Lucy into going to join Mike tomorrow,' she told Denzil, who stiffened.

'You promised to undo these handcuffs! Get them off me, will you? It's driving me crazy, being helpless like this.'

Clare gave him a cold, sardonic smile. 'I'm glad you've realised that at last!'

'What is that supposed to mean?'

'Now you know how your victims felt!'

His teeth showed between his curling lips. 'My victims! You've used that expression before, and I still don't know what the hell you're talking about.'

'Oh, no, of course you don't!'

'And you can drop the heavy sarcasm!' he snarled. 'If you have something to accuse me of, go ahead. Don't just drop vague hints.'

'You made Helen ill——'

'Helen made herself ill! She quarrelled with her husband and they got divorced, but she was still in love with him, and as miserable as sin. That was what made Helen ill. Not me.'

'She may have loved Paul all the time, but for a while she lost her head over you. She told me herself how helpless she felt, and I saw her with you, remember. I know the state she was in over you.'

He lowered his lids and watched her through his black lashes, his eyes like the silvery gleam of water through dark reeds.

'You seem to take a close interest in my relationships with other women.'

A flush crept into her face. She gave him an angry look. 'Helen is my friend, and Lucy is my sister.'

'Is it my fault if they both found me attractive?' he drawled, and she flared up again.

'You had them both hypnotised, like some vampire lover! They had stopped using their heads. Afterwards, when she was over you, Helen told me how she had felt... obsessed, unable to think of anything else, helpless to break away from you.'

She looked at him, suddenly laughing, but not in amusement, in pure, cold anger.

'As helpless as you are now!' she threw at him, and saw the way his face reacted. He didn't like that idea. A bitter undertone to her voice, Clare added, 'As helpless as I was downstairs, when you forced me against the wall and told me I was your prisoner.'

He lay very still, staring at her. She had all his attention now, she saw with angry cynicism.

'I was kidding, it was just a game!' he said slowly.

She sat down on the side of the bed. 'A game, was it? You touched me against my will, remember? Like this...' Slowly she ran her long index finger upwards over his naked chest and saw his entire body tense. '"Helpless" was the word you used—you said we were at war, and I was a helpless prisoner. Well, look who's the prisoner now. How does it feel?'

He looked stupefied.

She ran her finger lightly over his mouth. 'What's the matter? You seemed to think it was such a joke, downstairs. This game you were playing with me— I could see you were really enjoying yourself.' Lightly, she began to trace his features with that wandering finger: his cheekbones, his nose, his eyes, his brows. 'I was the toy you were playing with, wasn't I? You ignored all my protests, you just used me for one of your boy's games. Well, two can play games.'

His disbelief amused her. He couldn't believe this was happening to him! She bent, her blonde hair spilling around his face, to whisper into his ear, 'Now it's you who's the toy!' and softly bite his lobe.

She felt him wrenching at his handcuffs and laughed, looking into his furious, glittering eyes.

'What's the matter? Don't you like games any more?'

'OK, you've had your fun,' he bit out. 'Now unlock these damned things; I've had enough.'

'You may have, I haven't!' Clare said, feeling a dizzying sense of elation sweeping through her. She had looked into those hypnotic eyes of his and hadn't felt her will seeping away, or her mind cloud. Tied up like this he had lost his power over her.

'Clare! My patience is wearing thin!' he snapped, and she laughed at him.

'Is that supposed to make me tremble?'

She stretched out full-length on the bed, beside him, her head propped up on one hand while she looked down at his body through half-closed eyes, smiling to herself.

'It's an interesting experience, having a man entirely at my mercy. For most women it's usually the other way round. There's a lot of talk about equality, but men still have all the advantages— they're bigger, tougher, and the social rules favour them. I can't walk down a street at night, alone, without being afraid; I'd be wary of going back to a man's flat after a date, or being alone with him anywhere unless I'd known him for years and trusted him.' She almost absently put out a hand to him, ran it along his powerful shoulders and felt them tense under her caress. 'You're more muscular than I'd realised, just seeing you in your clothes. How do you keep fit? Gym? Sport?'

'Both,' he said shortly.

'I just walk; I do a lot of walking, in good weather, but only in daylight, and nowhere isolated—that's another drawback to being a woman; you never quite feel safe, even in your own home, if you're alone.'

She ran her fingers down his deep chest until she reached his hard brown nipples, softly drawing circles around them with an idle finger, hearing his intake of breath with a sense of triumph.

'Oh, you like that?' she whispered, smiling. He was watching her with fixed intensity now, his eyes dark, brilliantly glazed.

'I'd like it a lot more if I weren't trussed up like a chicken for the oven!'

She laughed, lowering her head, flicked her tongue over one of his nipples.

'If we're going to make love I want to have my hands free!' he muttered thickly.

She didn't bother to answer. Her hand was slowly running down over his flat stomach, his midriff, the rough-haired expanse below that. When she met the waistband of his pyjama trousers, she undid the button, and the fine black silk fell apart, freeing the erection her sensual caresses had caused.

He made a deep, harsh sound and turned dark red.

Clare couldn't stop staring.

In one part of her brain she was bewildered, amazed—she had never touched a man like this before. Oh, she'd made love with Hal, up to a point, and, indeed, with one or two others before him, but she had always been slow to burn, a cool, even inhibited girl who never quite gave herself completely, kept men slightly at a distance. Her outer image matched her inner self—cool, restrained, in total control of herself. But not any more.

Something seemed to have jammed the controls tonight. She felt wild quivers of sensation rushing through her and the more she gave in to her impulses, the stronger they became.

Slowly and deliberately her hand went out. Denzil groaned in his throat as she touched him. Clare watched her fingers brush clingingly upwards, feeling his hot flesh react, move with her, as if magnetised.

'For God's sake, Clare...' He swallowed. 'Please, unlock the cuffs; I can't stand this. I need to touch you, I want to hold you. Can't you see what you're doing to me?'

'I'm not blind,' she said, and her fingers trickled downwards.

He gave a hoarse gasp. 'Clare...' His dark eyes were enormous, glittering. 'Untie me,' he begged. 'We can't make love like this; it's sheer hell... I'm going out of my mind!'

'Good,' she whispered huskily, trembling with an unbearable fever. She hadn't intended to do any

of this; she was being swept away on a tide she
hadn't expected. She hadn't realised that desire
could be as disastrous and irresistible as any other
natural force.

Her body slid sideways, half on top of him, one
leg lying alongside his while the other pinned him
down. She felt him shuddering, heard the breath
rasping in his throat. Clare caressed him, almost
absently, bending towards his mouth, her hair tum-
bling around him.

Under the blonde curtain of her hair, he went on
watching her through his slitted lids, his lips apart,
not making a sound now—he hardly seemed to be
breathing.

Clare stopped just before their mouths touched.
She softly ran her hand downwards from his throat
to his thighs, feeling the clench of his taut muscles
under her caress.

'I think I want you,' she said conversationally,
and saw sweat spring out on his cheekbones.

He said something violent under his breath and
she laughed.

She was so hot that she shrugged off her jacket.
He watched it fall to the floor beside the bed; she
saw the black glitter of the pupils of his eyes, herself
reflected in them; saw the graining of his skin, a
haze of perspiration on his brow, a little muscle
pulling beside his mouth.

'Hot in here, isn't it?' she said in the same casual,
conversational tone, and knelt up, straddling him,
her knees grasping his waist. She lifted both arms
to pull her pale blue angora sweater off, over her
head, the movement tilting her high, round breasts,

straining them against the delicate white lace of her slip.

He watched with dilated eyes—she saw a pulse leaping in his neck.

His voice cracked like a whip. 'I'm losing my sense of humour, Clare! Get these handcuffs off me now!'

She undid the zip in her skirt and pulled that off over her head, then took off her slip; now she was only wearing her bra and panties.

Denzil was breathing as if he had just finished a marathon. 'I can't believe this is happening,' he grated. 'Maybe I'm dreaming . . . it can't be real, it must be a dream.'

'It isn't,' Clare said, and bit his neck.

He gave a sharp, pleasurable gasp. 'God! Clare . . . why are you doing this?'

'I haven't started doing it yet,' she said softly, and bent to trace his mouth with the tip of her tongue; slid it just between his parted lips and saw his eyes shut. He made a deep, raw noise and began to kiss her back passionately.

'Oh . . . yes . . . Clare, yes,' he breathed against her mouth, but she broke off the kiss at once, lifted her head again, to look at him.

This was not the man who had mocked her earlier, teased her and laughed at her all these months, played clever, sophisticated games with other women. His face looked very different: his eyes were closed, his skin taut over his clenched facial bones, his lips parted in gasping breath, desire like a death mask over his features.

He wasn't amused now. He wasn't the one in control, taking whatever he wanted, doing whatever he liked.

She remembered her dream of him on Christmas Eve in front of the fire—the black shadow swooping down like the black bat night engulfing her; the languid weakness, the piercing excitement she had felt and at last his mouth at her neck, and then a wild heat, a helplessness, the icy needle of intense desire as his lips parted on her skin and she felt the sting of his teeth biting her. It had been a sensation she could never forget, as if her life-blood was flowing into him. She had known then that that was what he did to women. He wasn't doing that to her.

This time he was the victim. This time she was doing that to him.

She reached round and unclipped her bra, let it fall. He opened his eyes to stare feverishly at her soft white flesh, the aroused pink nipples standing up from their delicate aureolae of brown pigment.

'You're so lovely,' he whispered in a voice that was shaking. 'I'm aching to kiss you, touch you . . . let me, Clare. Don't torture me.'

'I'm exorcising you,' she said, and lowered her head again.

He lifted his own head eagerly to meet her mouth, but she went for his neck. She heard his heartbeat race out of control just below her, his breathing fast and rough as her mouth parted on his throat.

He moaned, his body shuddering underneath her in a helpless response as she gently grazed his skin with her teeth, feeling the salt of his sweat on her tongue.

'What the hell do you mean, exorcising me? I wish I understood you, Clare. I've been dying to get my arms round you for months, don't you know that? And now you've got me tied up like this and I can't do a thing.'

Clare wasn't listening. She was moving against him, intensely aware of every movement he made in response, his hips lifting to meet hers, the restless shift of his thighs as he tried to manipulate her between them, pressing against her, struggling to get her closer.

Clare suddenly began to get scared. What was happening to her? What was this? It wasn't love; she wasn't in love with him—she couldn't be! She didn't even like him. But what was it—this hunger that ate her own insides, this need which was intolerable?

Why had she ever started this? She shouldn't have touched him. Each kiss, each touch had fed the furnace of desire inside her, sending her temperature climbing.

I've got to stop, she thought, but she didn't want to. Her eyes shut, she began sliding down his tense body like a slow, warm snake, coiling around him, her breasts brushing him, smooth against his rougher skin, feeling the dampness of his perspiration on her, hearing the thud of his heart under her cheek, the rough drag of his breathing, the smothered groans breaking out of him.

She ran her tongue around the inside of his navel, thinking that that had been where he had once been

tied to his mother. What had she been like, the
woman who had given him life? Clare felt a strong
curiosity about her; she wished she could meet her,
but maybe they would hate each other on sight.
Women who both loved a man often did—how
could they help fearing each other, resenting each
other, when they both wanted to be the only one
who possessed him?

She lay still, her face buried on him for a moment
as the realisation really hit her.

She wanted to possess this man. She hated every
other woman who had ever known him, every
woman he had ever touched, kissed, made love to.

'Don't stop,' he moaned, his hips twisting up
towards her.

She ran her hands down to his thighs and pushed
them apart, then her mouth slid downwards again
and a deep groan wrenched out of him.

'Clare...oh, this is pure torment. Undo the cuffs;
I've got to touch you, do this to you...please...'

Her tonguetip flicked and Denzil shuddered from
head to foot, making sounds that sent shock-waves
through her. Words didn't reach her but the driven
hunger in his voice did.

That was all she could respond to now. She had
stopped thinking. The fever consuming her made
it impossible to think. She was driven by primitive
instincts, sensual tides, her body in total command
of her.

She was naked now, and so was he, their bodies
clinging so intimately that you couldn't have got a
sheet of paper between them. Denzil's thighs imprisoned her, held her down on top of him.

Her breathing almost tore her apart as she felt him pushing up against her, the ribbed column searching like a heat-seeking missile for its target.

'First . . . darling . . . let me out of these cuffs,' he muttered, but she didn't answer. Confused and dizzy, she couldn't think how she had got to this point; this wasn't what she had had in mind in the beginning. This had all started when she'd seen she had him in her power, and felt a surge of elation. Ever since the first time she saw him she had been half afraid of him, very aware of his power over women, secretly terrified of coming under his power herself. She had spent the last months fighting the way he made her feel, and when she'd seen him handcuffed to the bed and unable to do a thing to her she had gone crazy.

Now her body was out of control and it was too late to stop what was happening. The taste of power was heady; she was already addicted to it. She needed what his body was trying to give her. Her eyes shut, she slowly sank on to him, and Denzil gave a long, thick groan.

'Clare.'

For a moment they were both still. Clare breathed, feeling him inside her, filling her; then she slowly began to move again, and heard his breathing quicken.

Her body drove for its own satisfaction, perspiration on her face, between her breasts, as she began to feel the slow tremors of agonised pleasure build. Her face was tilted up, her mouth open, eyes closed, her bones locked into a mask of frenzied desire.

It was like free-falling, without a parachute, through rushing air. She was lost, crying out, sobbing, her body utterly helpless in the slow, burning rhythm possessing her.

When it was over she lay still for a few seconds, tears on her face, aware of Denzil still moving inside her, his mouth against her hair, his cheek rubbing against hers.

Clare took a long breath, rubbed a hand over her wet face, and withdrew from him.

He gave a sharp, incredulous, furious cry. 'What are you doing? Clare . . . you can't stop now . . .'

She rolled away, face averted, scrambled off the bed, almost falling over because her legs gave way as she stood up.

Denzil was darkly flushed, trembling violently, breathing in that tortured fashion, his chest rising and falling with the fierce intake of his breath.

Clare turned her back on him and began dressing in a tearing hurry, her hands shaky.

'You can't,' Denzil broke out hoarsely. 'You can't do this to me! My God, what sort of woman are you? Clare! Are you listening? You seduce me, practically rape me, take me almost to the point of orgasm and then you calmly stop? If this is some sort of joke, I'm not laughing.' He stopped, took another thick breath, then angrily snapped, 'Are you hoping to hear me beg? You want me desperate enough to beg . . . is that it? Well, I'm not going to.'

She had difficulty doing up the zip of her skirt; she was almost fully dressed again, except for her tights, and she decided not to put them back on.

Denzil's voice changed again. 'This is another game, right? You're teasing me. You couldn't be cruel enough to work me up like this and then just walk away, leaving me going crazy with frustration!'

She flinched, biting her lip, and averted her face. She couldn't blame him for being so angry, but she wasn't making love to him again. She was furious with herself for ever having touched him. She knelt down and fumbled under the bed for the belt and chain she had hidden there.

Denzil watched her, his face drawn and furious. 'Now what are you doing?'

She stood up, dragging the chain on to the bed. It was heavy and rattled as she lifted it.

When he saw what she held, he tensed; she saw his stomach muscles contract, his body clench.

'What the hell is that?'

She didn't answer. She sat down on the edge of the bed and began sliding the belt underneath him.

'Clare, this has gone too far! Stop it, for God's sake!' He tried to stop her, pushing his body downwards to trap her hand between his body and the mattress. 'You swore you'd let me go if I made that call!'

She shook her head. 'I promised to take the handcuffs off. I never said I was going to let you go. Do you think I'm stupid? I know I can't trust you not to ring Lucy up again and tell her I made you cancel the film test.'

She caught the gleam of thought in his eyes. He quickly said, 'If you stay with me, I won't be able to, will I?'

'I'll be back,' she promised. 'I won't leave you chained up any longer than I have to.'

'You aren't leaving me chained up at all!' He was white with rage, his body rigid.

'I'm sorry, but there's no alternative. I can't trust you any other way. If you want me to unlock your handcuffs, and untie your feet, you'll have to let me put this belt on you; I've fixed the chain to the bed with a double padlock; you won't be able to break it or unlock it but I've made sure the chain stretches to the bathroom, so you shouldn't have too uncomfortable a time, and as soon as Lucy is out of the country I'll set you free.'

'What if she refuses to go to join her fiancé?'

'She won't.'

He studied the determined set of Clare's features, his mouth twisting. 'No, I suppose she won't, if you've made up your mind she's going. My God, you're tough, aren't you? Hard as nails and, in spite of the little performance you just put on for me, an iceberg, sexually. You were just having your own peculiar idea of fun at my expense, weren't you? Tormenting me, and never intending to follow through.' His voice was harsh, vibrating with bitter anger. 'If there's one sort of woman I can't stand it's a cold-blooded little tease.'

Clare paled, hating the tone he'd used, but she fought to keep any expression out of her face. She wouldn't give him the pleasure of knowing he had hurt her.

Watching her, he asked tersely, 'No comment?'

She looked back at him without expression; to do so was far from easy but she managed it somehow. 'No.'

His mouth hard, he nodded. 'As I said, cold as ice. You put on quite an act. You really turned me on, but that was what you meant to do, wasn't it? You knew exactly what you were doing.'

'We haven't got time for this,' Clare said curtly.

'You haven't,' he said through his clenched teeth. 'Apparently I've got all the time in the world. I'm not going anywhere.'

'Look, Lucy has to get on a train to Manchester at six o'clock tomorrow morning, and before she can do that she has to pack. And I still have to talk to her because she doesn't know anything about this trip.'

'Won't she need a visa?'

Clare was trying not to look at him; it sent vibrations through her every time she did. He was still naked, his lean, hard body a magnet to her eyes if she so much as glanced in his direction.

Flatly she said, 'She got one months ago, when Mike first went out there, so that if she ever saved up enough she could visit him.'

'What about him? When are you going to tell him she's coming?'

'I already have.'

Coldly derisive, he said, 'You amaze me. You're so secretive I'm surprised you told anyone what you were up to.'

She flushed, lifting her chin. 'I didn't tell him anything about you, or the film test—I just told him it was a surprise for Lucy, and warned him not to mention it to her in advance, but I had to let him know she was coming so that he could meet her at the airport, and book her into a hotel near him.'

'You thought of everything, didn't you?' he said drily, studying her like someone observing an insect under a microscope.

'I tried.' Clare looked impatiently at her watch. 'Now, are you going to let me put this belt on you or not? Because if you won't I'll leave you handcuffed all night.'

'Oh, put your damned belt on, by all means!' He lifted his body, freeing her hand, and she rapidly slid the belt right round his waist.

'Before I unlock your handcuffs I want your word that you won't try to stop me leaving,' she said, still without looking at him. 'I have to see Lucy tonight, make sure she gets that plane.'

'I'll give you my word in exchange for yours,' he drawled. 'You are coming back as soon as Lucy's on that train tomorrow morning?'

She nodded. 'Yes, I give you my word I'll be here immediately after seeing Lucy on the train.'

'Then it's a deal,' he said.

Not quite certain she could trust him, Clare took a deep breath, and unlocked the handcuffs.

His arms fell, he winced, gave a grunt of pain. 'My God, I've got the most terrible cramp.' He began rubbing his arms.

Clare hadn't waited around. In spite of his promise she was taking no chances. As soon as she had unlocked the handcuffs she got up, taking the phone with her, and began making for the door very fast. She heard him sitting up, shifting on the bed, but he couldn't catch her once she was out of arm's reach; his legs were still tied and he had to stop to untie the washing-line, which was not easy as she had gone to considerable lengths to make the knots difficult to untie.

'I'll be back very early in the morning; get some sleep,' she said over her shoulder.

Denzil said something very rude. She ignored it.

When she got back home she went up to her own room first. She didn't get undressed, she sat on her bed, listening to the muffled sounds of crying from Lucy's bedroom. After a minute she went in there and put on the light.

Lucy shot up on the bed, childish in a pink cotton nightshirt printed with teddy bears, but a tragic figure too, white-faced and tear-stained. 'What did you do that for?'

Clare sat down on the bed next to her and pulled a paper tissue from the box of them on her sister's bedside table. She gently began drying Lucy's eyes.

'What's wrong? I heard you crying.'

Lucy's lips trembled; she flared up but with less than her usual spirit. 'Have you been eaves-dropping again? Can't I even cry in peace in this house?' Then she gave a little wail. 'Oh, Clare…the film test has been cancelled. He's going away again, and I'm never going to be in films, after all.'

'I'm not surprised,' Clare said with all honesty, picking up a hairbrush from the dressing-table and running it over her sister's tousled hair. 'I think that film test gag is something he tries on all the women he chases.'

Lucy had always loved having her hair brushed; it soothed her. She sighed. 'You were right about him.'

'Yes.' Clare had the air ticket in her pocket. She pulled it out. 'Well, then, maybe you can use this...'

Lucy looked blankly at it as if it were a rabbit Clare had pulled out of a hat. 'What is it?'

'Open it and see.'

Lucy took it uncertainly, opened it, tried to read it. 'A flight to Africa! I don't understand—this is for tomorrow morning! But——'

'If you don't want to go tomorrow you can change the date, if you let them know in advance, but I have rung Mike and warned him you're coming.'

'You rang Mike?' Lucy was open-mouthed, incredulous. 'You told him...when? When did you buy the ticket? When did you talk to Mike? What is all this?'

Clare kept her cool, shrugged, smiled at her. 'Does any of that matter? You haven't got much time to make up your mind. You've got a seat booked on a train early tomorrow, and Mike has booked you into a hotel near the school; everything is arranged. All you have to do is pack a case and catch that train.'

Lucy stared at her fixedly, frowning. 'When did you do all this?'

'A couple of days ago.'

'But...why? Without telling me? What's been going on?'

'I told you at the time, I never did believe in that film test stuff; I was sure it was just a line he was spinning.'

Lucy bit her lip. 'You must think I'm an idiot.'

Clare smiled lovingly at her. 'No, you just ran into an emotional vampire who was way out of your league. That guy has a history of preying on unhappy women; he starts out being sweetly sympathetic and supportive and ends up in their beds. When he's got what he wanted from them he flaps on somewhere else.'

Lucy giggled nervously.

'Isn't that what happened with you?' asked Clare. 'You were unhappy over Mike and he moved in on you, so understanding, so soothing, how could you help liking him? Then he started trying to get you into bed.'

Lucy blushed. 'I never told you that!'

'It wasn't hard to guess,' Clare said grimly. 'He's predictable. I was certain he had no intention of putting you in his film, and I was worried about how you would take it when the film test fell through; I was afraid it would be the last straw after your trouble with Mike, so I started making these arrangements. If you did have a film test I could have rung and changed the date to some later time, so it wasn't much of a risk. You need a holiday, Lucy; you've been overworking, and I think you need to see Mike and talk things over with him, too. You can't do that on the phone, or by letter. You have to see him, face to face.'

Lucy bit her lip, undecided, flushed, her fair hair dishevelled. 'I don't know what to say.'

'Just say you'll go!' Clare teased.

Lucy hugged her, half sobbing. 'You're wonderful; I'm so grateful, Clare...I'll never forget this...'

'I just want you to be happy, Lucy. I think you and Mike are right for each other, and he'll make you very happy. I didn't want you to lose him just for the sake of an air fare, and now that the business is doing so well I could afford to send you. Now, are you going to pack now or try to sleep and pack in the morning?'

'Pack now,' said Lucy. 'I can catch up with my sleep on the train tomorrow.'

She leapt out of bed, filled with energy, flushed and excited. Clare helped her; it only took them both half an hour, then Clare made Lucy go back to bed.

'I'll wake you in good time to get that train,' she promised, putting out the light.

She went into her own bedroom and lay down, fully dressed, on the bed, staring into the darkness. She had felt no compunction about lying to her sister; if she had told Lucy the truth she knew Lucy wouldn't have got on that plane and Clare was convinced that Mike was the right man for her sister.

She was just as convinced that Lucy wasn't missing out on a great career by not doing that film test. Lucy was quite lovely, it was true, and photogenic—Clare knew she always looked stunning in photographs—but Lucy had never shown any particular acting talent. She had often done school plays, but she had no stage charisma, or none that Clare had ever noticed. Denzil hadn't pretended to believe she might have star quality, either. He had said he'd offered her a film test out of the kindness of his heart, but Clare was sure she was right about his motives—he had used it as bait to get Lucy into bed. No doubt it was a well-worn tactic with him, and presumably it worked with most girls. Obviously it hadn't worked with Lucy—yet. But it might have done if Lucy's engagement had been broken off.

She frowned at the ceiling, her face pale and cold. She shouldn't have started thinking about him. Now that she wasn't keeping busy, had nothing else to think about, her head began to fill with disturbing images.

She couldn't believe what she remembered doing... Had she really behaved like that, touched him like that? What on earth had possessed her?

Her own intrinsic honesty, the bedrock quality of her nature, wouldn't let her lie to herself. Now that she was alone in the dark she couldn't pretend not to know or understand the truth about her feelings for him. She closed her eyes, moaning, anguish and desire choking her, tearing at her inside, as if she had swallowed broken glass.

She was in love with him. Hopelessly. How could she have been so stupid?

He had called her crazy tonight, and he was right, she had to be out of her mind to fall for someone like him.

Why on earth had she taken so long to realise what was happening to her? She had a good brain, but it had failed her this time.

Of course, she had been blinded by the hostility she had felt from the minute they first met, never recognising that it was a mere smoke-screen for something far more dangerous. She had been so full of concern for Helen that first night, on the surface, seeing Denzil as an emotional vampire who would only hurt Helen and walk away without a second's thought.

Now she wondered if she had always secretly suspected that she herself was at risk from him too.

Oh, but she had always been cool and sensible: a good businesswoman, level-headed and down-to-earth. She had told herself that no man would ever hurt her again, that her heartbreak over Hal had cured her of falling for the wrong sort of man, but looking back she wondered if she hadn't known on sight that Denzil Black could threaten her peace of mind, that his effect on her could be cataclysmic. Why else had she been so terrified of him? Why had she had all those disturbing dreams about him?

She had managed to rescue her sister from him— but who was going to rescue her?

## CHAPTER SEVEN

CLARE was intensely nervous as she drove up to her cottage next morning in a pale golden light. Spring was definitely here, and it looked as if it was going to be a beautiful day, not a cloud in sight, and blue hyacinths had begun to open their tight, curled petals, right next to the front door, their scent so strong that it was heady. Clare paused to inhale the fragrance, knowing that she was delaying the moment when she had to go inside, up the stairs.

She had seen Lucy on to her train then driven straight here, but very slowly, her face pale with apprehension. She couldn't keep him chained up, but she was terrified of what he might do to her once he was free.

She bit her lip, her pale face turning scarlet as she remembered last night. How could she blame him if he thought, after the way she'd behaved, that she would be ready to jump into bed with him at the first opportunity? He was going to be expecting...

She groaned aloud. Oh, why did I do it? What on earth possessed me?

Well, that was it, wasn't it? She *was* possessed. Ever since the first time she set eyes on Denzil she had been possessed, if by that you meant taken over, obsessed, her mind overwhelmed by strange images, her dreams sensual, haunting, disturbing.

151

In the Middle Ages they had called it being possessed by the devil, and that description seemed apt for Denzil.

'Vampire lover, demon lover,' she muttered aloud, then stopped, closed her eyes and leaned her face on the stone wall. I am going out of my mind. I talk to myself, I have hallucinations, I have the weirdest dreams... What is wrong with me? Apart from being in love with the last man in the world that any sane woman would ever fall in love with?

'Oh, shut up!' she said aloud, talking to herself again. There was no point in standing out here arguing about it—she had to go inside and face what was waiting for her.

She put the key in the lock, opened the door and stood in the little hallway, listening.

Not a sound. She quietly closed the door behind her and began tiptoeing up the stairs, pausing every few steps to listen again.

When she reached the landing she heard him breathing. Clare stood there, a pulse beating in her throat, registering the quiet, regular sound. He was asleep.

She might be able to sneak in there and put the key down near him without waking him up, then run for it.

Relief made her feel almost sick. The bedroom door was slightly open; she very carefully pushed it back and saw him a second later, with a leap of the heart.

He was lying on his back, on the bed, his eyes closed, black lashes barring his pale cheeks, his mouth open, breathing audibly through it. The quilt was carelessly draped over the lower half of his body, his chest and shoulders bare. The curtains were drawn, the room shadowy.

But what if he wasn't really asleep? What if he was only pretending, to trap her?

She took another look at him. No, if he were acting he wouldn't have his mouth that wide open.

Clare began to creep towards him, intending to put the key on his bedside table and creep out again, but when she was halfway across the room he shifted restlessly, and she froze, watching him, ready to bolt if he sat up.

His eyelids flickered, he breathed rapidly, in a shallow way, then began to groan, twisting his head from side to side. Clare couldn't hear what he was muttering—the words were blurred, hoarse—but then he cried out in a way that scared the life out of her.

She had never heard fear, almost anguish, in a man's voice before. She was so upset that she ran to the bed and sat down on it, shook him violently. 'Wake up, Denzil!'

His breathing altered, he grunted in a sort of shock, then his eyes flew open. He stiffened, looking up at her dazedly. For a minute she was sure he did not know who she was, then he stammered, 'W-what's wrong... ? Clare?'

Shakily she said, 'You were having a bad dream... a nightmare...'

If anything he turned paler, his skin waxy, his eyes very dark. 'How do you know? What did I say?'

She saw with incredulity that he was embarrassed; it didn't fit with the man she knew, but instinctively she reassured him. 'You weren't talking, you were yelling.' She could empathise; whatever he had been dreaming about must have been a very private vision—it had sounded like a vision of hell, and he wouldn't want anyone to know what was giving him nightmares like that.

He sighed heavily, put his arm across his face in a gesture she found intensely touching. He looked so much like a little boy trying to hide that before she knew what she meant to do she was stroking the tousled black hair back from his forehead, murmuring softly.

'You're OK now, it's all over, you're awake, it's morning.'

In a voice she only just heard he grated, 'It's never over—things like that never are; they come back in dreams, over and over again, when you're asleep and your defences are down.'

Startled and uncertain, Clare hesitated. 'It sounds bad. Do you want to talk about it?'

He laughed harshly. 'What are you expecting? Something horrific and terrifying? No, Clare. My nightmares are nothing unusual or special—just ordinary childhood horrors I should have grown out of long ago.'

For a second she felt relief, but then she remembered the sounds he had made and frowned, realising that, whether he called it ordinary or not, his horror had been real and unbearable.

'Did you have a bad childhood?' She was aware of walking on thin ice, each step needing to be worked out carefully in advance. She already knew him well enough to be sure he wasn't the type to want to talk about his private feelings, any more than she was. With a sting of surprise it occurred to her for the first time that they were in some ways alike.

After a long silence Denzil muttered roughly, 'It had bad moments.'

She took a deep breath, startled by her own pleasure because he had actually answered, told her that much. She felt like someone who had managed to persuade a wild bird to take food from her hand.

Carefully, she asked in a voice she made as casual as possible, 'Didn't you get on with your parents?'

He laughed angrily, lowering his arm and looking at her with hard grey eyes. 'My parents? When I was two years old, my mother ran off with another man and my father didn't know what to do with me, so he dumped me on his sister and vanished, too. His sister had four children of her own, all boys, in their teens when I arrived. To say they didn't want me around is a vast understatement. They made it their business to see that my life was hell, and they had vivid imaginations.'

She winced. 'You mean they bullied you?'

'They thought of a hundred different ways of making a small boy wish he had never been born.'

Clare was appalled, watching him with darkened eyes. 'But... why didn't you tell someone... your aunt, their mother? Why didn't you tell her?'

Cynicism tightened his face. 'They were clever; they didn't leave marks, except on my mind, and my aunt Flora never saw what she didn't want to see. She hadn't wanted me either, of course. She was a widow, without that much money; she took me in simply because, as she told me a dozen times a day, it was her duty. She was a religious woman, strong on duty, short on human affections, except where her own children were concerned. Oh, she saw to it that I was fed and clothed and taken to church once a week. She herself wasn't cruel, merely indifferent. Things weren't so bad when the boys were at school, but weekends and holidays were terrifying to me. I particularly hated Christmas, when they were all home but because of bad weather didn't spend much time out of doors. That meant they were indoors—amusing themselves with me. They endlessly played what they called practical jokes on me—when people call them practical jokes they really mean cruel jokes, you know. There's always some cruelty involved. The victim never enjoys the joke.'

'I know what you mean,' Clare said slowly. 'I hate having practical jokes played on me, too. What sort of things did they do to you?'

He grimaced. 'Oh, petty, spiteful tricks—but when you're four years old they can seem like tortures. The Christmas I was five, they filled my bed with pine needles, from the tree, and forced me to get into it. It wasn't agonising, but they scratched and stung, like nettles. Sometimes they pushed me into the cupboard under the stairs and locked me in; it was always pitch-dark in there and I was petrified. I've had a touch of claustrophobia ever since. They habitually hid my presents, or threw them around until they broke, then they made me

take the blame. My aunt believed in strict punish-
ments; she beat me all the time for things her sons
had done. I remember one game they liked a lot—
they called it Crumpets. They all held me over the
fire and pretended to toast me. They never actually
let me fall, but I was never quite sure they wouldn't.
In fact, that mental cruelty was typical; it wasn't
so much what they did as what I thought they might
do next. They twisted my arms, and pulled my hair,
whenever they saw me, just as casually as they
might kick a dog.'

Very pale, Clare had to fight to keep back tears;
the image of a small, motherless boy having to bear
all this made her both angry and deeply distressed.

'How long did you have to put up with all this?'
she asked huskily, and he grimaced.

'It seemed like eternity, but in fact it was about
five or six years, I suppose—by the time I was eight,
they had all left school, they were either at work,
or at college, and they'd grown bored with the fun
of tormenting me.'

'I can see why you say you hate Christmas,' she
thought aloud.

He gave her a quick, sideways look. 'Did I tell
you that?'

She nodded.

He smiled crookedly. 'Yes, well, Christmas was
the worst time of the year for me. I hated the con-
trast between their mother's talk about loving one
another and leading a good life, and what her sons
were doing to me behind her back, while she turned
a blind eye to it.'

Appalled, Clare broke out, 'How could she do that?'

'She didn't want to know, I suppose. Don't mothers always prefer to believe their children are perfect? Especially at Christmas time. I learnt to hate that whole season—the church services, the carol concerts, the Christmas cards with their loving messages, the holly and tinsel. The whole world seems to be full of families getting together; there are nothing but nostalgic old films on TV...endless carols on radio...you can't get away from it wherever you go, but for me everything about it was phoney.'

'I can see why you'd think that.'

She didn't try to argue; this was not the time or place to make him see Christmas any other way. Gently, she said, 'No wonder you have nightmares. What happens to you as a child seems to make more impression than anything that happens in the rest of your life, doesn't it?'

'Apparently,' he growled, his eyes sardonic. 'Stupid, isn't it? It's nearly twenty years since my aunt died, and I haven't seen any of my cousins since. I should have forgotten what they did to me, but...' He shrugged, then said flatly, 'Oddly enough she died at Christmas, suddenly, of a heart attack. Nobody realised she had a weak heart; it was a shock...' Then he stopped dead, very pale, his brows black. 'No,' he said harshly. 'That isn't the whole truth. I've never told anyone this, but the real fact is, it was my fault; I made her have that heart attack. My cousins were coming on Christmas Day...two of them were married and had kids of their own, and they were bringing their families, the other two were bringing girlfriends, and my aunt was over the moon. She kept going on about what a wonderful family time Christmas was and what wonderful sons she had, and I suddenly lost my temper and told her what cruel little brutes her sons had been to me, how much I hated them——'

He broke off, breathing raggedly, and Clare saw his hands shaking. She took them both and held them, horrified by the look on his face.

He stared down at their linked hands, then shot a look up at her.

'Are you being kind and sympathetic to me, Clare?'

She went pink at what she heard as dry sarcasm and tried to pull her hands away, but he held on to them.

'No, I wasn't getting at you. It's just that I've often played this scene the other way around—it's usually me being a good listener, letting people talk their problems out, not this way around. Quite often, that's a big part of a director's job, especially when you're working with temperamental, emotional actors.'

'And especially if they're beautiful actresses?' Clare suggested drily and got a glinting, amused look.

'Miaow.'

She flushed a darker pink. Had he picked up the secret jealousy in her tone? She could kick herself.

Denzil added wryly, 'I must say, it's a new experience to be on this side of the camera for once, but I don't want to bore you with my self-pitying reminiscences. There's nothing so tedious as someone else's childhood memories.'

'You aren't boring me!' she assured him, and meant it.

He made a face. 'I suppose I'm reluctant to tell you any more because it doesn't show me in a very good light.' He paused, frowning, then said curtly, 'I wanted to hurt my aunt. That's the unforgivable part of what happened. I was angry because she was so happy and pleased with herself and her boys... I kept remembering what Christmas had always been like for me, the odd one out in that house, the one they either ignored or picked on... I felt this terrible rush of rage and I shouted the truth at her. I was in that teenage phase when you turn righteous; I felt justified in shoving the truth into her face. Of course she wouldn't believe it. Or admit it, anyway. She started shouting back at me... and suddenly began to choke and clutch at her chest. She staggered and fell back into a chair. I was frightened; I bent over her to ask if she was OK, and she hit me. That was her last act.' He lifted his head again and looked at Clare, his face white. 'The last thing she ever did was hit me, and then she died, and I didn't try to help her.'

Clare had an overwhelming impulse to put her arms around him, but she was scared of doing that, so she tightened her grip on his hands. 'You must have been very frightened. Only a teenager and feeling guilty... I don't suppose you even knew what to do?'

'I didn't have a clue, actually. She was making this terrible noise one minute, the next she'd stopped breathing.' He looked at Clare fixedly, his eyes very dark. 'I didn't even try to help her, that's what I can never forget. I just stood there, staring; it was as if time had stopped. That last blow had made me...I don't know...numb, I suppose. It seemed so typical...that the last thing she did was hit me.'

'You were in shock,' Clare said gently.

'I suppose I was. All I know is I just stood there, gaping, then I panicked. I didn't try to give her first aid, I just ran and rang for an ambulance. The doctor who came with the ambulance told me she had died instantly, but I've never been sure he was right.'

'You were only a kid, Denzil! It isn't surprising that you panicked.'

'I don't know. Maybe if I'd done something...tried artificial respiration, tried to get her heart beating again. She might have survived if I'd done the right thing. I'll never know now.'

Clare felt like crying. His eyes were such deep, dark wells of pain. 'And you've felt guilty ever since,' she whispered.

He gave her a twisted smile. 'I've tried to forget about her ever since, but you're right, I did feel guilty. So I should. After all, she did give me a home, she didn't have to do that, and it wasn't she who treated me badly. It was her sons, who are now perfectly respectable members of society, by the way, I gather. It was my bad luck that they were in the thug phase of teenage when I turned up; you know adolescents usually go through a period of ganging up on other kids, just for kicks. My aunt couldn't be blamed for that, any more than she could be blamed because she didn't have any affection to spare after having had four sons of her own.'

They sat in silence for a moment, then Clare asked, 'What happened to you after your aunt died?'

'My father was dead by then—he was lost at sea, a couple of years earlier, working on a cruise liner. I think he jumped overboard, but officially it was an accident; he had been drinking at the time.'

'What about your mother?'

'God knows where she is—she may be dead too, for all I know. Or care. She just disappeared when I was two and nobody has seen or heard of her since. My cousins inherited everything their mother left, of course. It wasn't much, just the house, and a few other items. They sold the house and divided the money between them, so I was left homeless.'

Clare flinched from the bleakness in his voice, the bleakness of everything he had told her. It explained so much about him; all the things she had sensed from the minute they met: a mysterious remoteness, a distance from the human warmth of ordinary life, and a sense, too, of him watching, from outside, from the dark, through the lighted windows of other people's lives. Denzil had always been an outsider.

Gently she asked, 'What happened to you next, then?'

'I had my first real piece of luck.' His grey eyes glinted with a frosty amusement. 'I have a theory, by the way, about life, the universe and everything.

I suppose you could say I believe in a balancing of the books. If you get a run of very bad luck, sooner or later your luck turns; you can call it what you like, God, providence, compensation, the see-saw theory, or what goes up must come down, and vice versa, but one day your luck turns. I'd had a very bad deal from life until I was almost an adult, but from the day my aunt died my luck changed. One of my teachers offered me a home until I was eighteen. She was a very different type from my aunt; she had children too, but they were all grown up and living away from home, and she and her husband liked having young people around the house.'

His face had changed, softened, warmed. It made him look so different.

'They sound wonderful,' Clare said tentatively.

He smiled. 'They were. The Durrells were blessed with young minds and young hearts; in fact, they still are, and they're over seventy, both of them, now. My life changed completely from the day I moved in with them. They got me into college, and I did a film course, which was how I started on my career. I still see them from time to time; I've always kept in touch.'

'And your cousins?'

His face tightened again. Curtly he said, 'I've never seen them since.' He paused then added, 'And I try never to think of them. I don't have those dreams very often any more, but if I'm very tired, or under pressure, or something is bothering me, the dreams start up again.'

Clare was stricken suddenly. She turned white and felt sick.

'Oh...' It hadn't occurred to her until that moment; now she said, 'You...you had it just now because I'd chained you to the bed...that's why, isn't it?'

He shrugged and didn't answer, but he didn't have to—Clare was realising what that must have done to him after the cruelties his cousins had practised on him all those years.

'I'm sorry...so sorry...if I'd known I'd never have...' she stammered. 'Why on earth didn't you tell me you suffered from claustrophobia? It must have been a nightmare for you——' She broke off, bit her lower lip.

He laughed. 'Would you have believed me?'

She groaned. 'Probably not.' Her hand shaking, she pulled the key out of her jacket pocket, said breathlessly, 'Sit up and I'll unlock the belt.'

He sat up, his black silk pyjama-top open to the waist. Clare was so upset that it took her a minute to turn the lock, but at last he was free. She dropped the belt and chain, rattling, on to the floor beside the bed.

He stretched, made a deep sound of relief. 'Thank heavens for that. It was damned uncomfortable.'

Huskily she said, 'I'm sorry, I never meant to hurt you; I was only trying to——'

'Save your sister from me, I know,' he said drily. 'Lucy's on her way now, I presume? What time is her plane?'

She gave him a secretive, uncertain glance through her lashes. She might feel sorry for him, after hearing about his terrible childhood, but she wasn't absolutely sure she trusted him. She wouldn't be surprised if he took reprisals for what she had done. She was ready to run if he tried to grab her, but so far he had made no threatening moves in her direction.

'I did the right thing, you know!' she told him. 'She does love Mike; she'll be happy with him.'

'You don't have to justify yourself to me. It's Lucy whose life you've manipulated.'

Her flush deepened, her old impatience with him coming back. 'Oh, come on, admit it—there was never any real chance of a big film career for her, was there?'

He shrugged and looked sardonic again. 'I doubt it. She is beautiful, and she would have looked good, but I'm fairly sure she can't act, having worked with her on the pageant. I watched her trying to show the kids how to act and she's pretty wooden, I'm afraid.'

'I know, I remember her in school plays—she looked wonderful and she spoke the lines very clearly, but ... well, she wasn't really very good.'

'She doesn't have enough imagination to make an actress,' Denzil said. 'Or enough humility or inner doubt. She's too pleased with her own lovely self to want to be someone else, and a good actress needs to want that. Usually you find they're riddled with self-doubts and desperately looking for reassurance.'

'Why did you suggest a test, if you knew she was no good?'

'She wasn't happy and I'd almost run out of sympathetic noises to make when she talked about her troubles. I thought it would be fun for her to have a test; it might take her mind off her own problems for a day or two, and if she was as photogenic as I suspected she'd have made a lovely piece of mosaic in my jigsaw.'

'A piece in your jigsaw,' Clare said slowly, a spot of red in each cheek.

He gave her a dry look, picking up the note in her voice. 'The overall picture I try to build,' he expanded. 'I see each frame like a painting, as you probably gathered from the story-board sketches you've seen here; every detail has to have a reason for being there, even if it is only to be convincing for that period or place, or just look good, and Lucy certainly does that.'

Clare was breathing quickly, her hands clenched.

He eyed her thoughtfully. 'You're angry again!'

'You almost ruined Lucy's life, and you talk about her being a piece of mosaic! Of course I'm angry, what do you expect?' Then she remembered what he had just told her about his childhood and stopped short, biting her lip, then said crossly, 'I suppose you can't help being so manipulative; you've never learnt to care about other people.'

'Don't try psycho-babble on me, Clare! I do care about other people, or I wouldn't have been sorry for Lucy. I knew she was unhappy, because she told me all her troubles; she talked to me for hours at a time, about Mike and marriage and her problems at school, her problems with you and the family, what she thought about everything, and I listened, which was all she wanted me to do. She just wanted to talk without being told what to do all the time.'

Furiously, Clare snapped, 'Is that a dig at me?'

'Well, you did try to run her life, didn't you? As you just proved by railroading her on to a plane to join her fiancé, and going to enormous lengths to get your own way too—even to chaining me up like a dog for hours on end!'

'I said I was sorry about that!'

'Are you sorry you drove me out of my mind with frustration, too?' he asked and the darkness in his eyes set alarm bells ringing inside her head.

She leapt off the bed. 'I've got to get to work . . .'

She didn't manage to take so much as a step. Denzil's hand grabbed her waist and yanked her back towards the bed. She tried to pull away but only succeeded in sprawling helplessly across him, a cry of panic coming out of her at the instant of contact.

Denzil's arm went round her and at the same moment he did a sort of crocodile roll, which ended up with her on her back on the bed and Denzil on top of her.

She was shaken by the pleasure she felt at feeling his body pressing her down into the bed.

'I'll kill you . . .' she began, and he looked down at her through his half-closed lids, smiling tormentingly . . .

'Will you? With most women I wouldn't believe a threat like that, but you're a very unusual woman. I think I recognised that the first time we met. I felt an odd sensation in the pit of my stomach as I looked at you. You're so passionate, Clare. I thought for a long time that there was just ice in your veins, but, my God, I was wrong, wasn't I? Last night I felt the hot blood beating inside you...here...' He bent suddenly and she gave a sharp cry as his lips drifted down her neck, making her shiver and tremble. 'And here,' he whispered, pushing aside the lapels of her white blouse and kissing the deep hollow between her breasts.

Her heart was beating so fast that she couldn't breathe. It was pure torture to be so close to him, feel his mouth caress her. She was on fire; she wanted him so much that she was going crazy; desire flared and leapt inside her but she didn't want him to make love to her when she knew he wasn't in love, was merely aroused because of last night, and determined to get her into bed. He made love brilliantly; every touch, every kiss undermined her, but she could still think. She knew about Denzil's capacity to seduce. She had watched him playing games with other women...with Helen...with her sister.

He wasn't playing games with her.

'I won't,' she muttered, struggling, hitting out at him. 'Let me go, will you? I don't want you...'

He lay still, looking down at her flushed face and restless eyes, the tremor in her mouth.

'Liar,' he whispered. 'Do you think I can't feel what's going on inside you now? Do you think I've forgotten the way you tormented me last night?' He caught her hand and drew it down between them, pushed it against his body and held it there, hearing her fierce intake of breath and watching scarlet flare into her face.

'Don't!'

'You didn't really think you could arouse me to the pitch of madness, then walk away, leaving me frustrated all night, without paying for it?' he asked harshly, and she flinched.

'I—I didn't mean to...arouse you...I didn't intend to touch you at all,' she stammered.

'But you did, Clare! Whether you claim you meant to or not!'

'I lost my temper!'

'You didn't touch me in anger!' he threw back at her, his body tense.

'I started to,' she protested. 'And then...' She couldn't finish that sentence. She could hardly breathe.

He was quick to pick up the quiver in her voice. 'And then?'

Clare muttered huskily, 'Once I started I couldn't...'

She felt his body moving against her restlessly, heard the intake of his breath. 'Couldn't what, Clare?'

'Stop,' she whispered, face burning.

'You wanted it as much as I did!' His voice was rough, with triumph, with excitement, with desire; she couldn't look at him, her eyes down, her face quivering.

'OK, I got carried away! But I didn't mean to let that happen; I'm not the type, I've never liked casual sex...'

'There was nothing casual about last night,' he said, and her skin was so hot that she felt she was in flames.

'Oh, shut up! Stop talking about it. I lost my head, I went a little crazy, but it didn't mean anything and . . . and it isn't happening again, ever, so just leave me alone. I've got to go to work; I have an agency to run. If I don't open up my family will get worried and start looking for me, and they'll undoubtedly come here!'

Denzil shifted as if to get up and she waited tensely, hoping he was going to be reasonable, ready to jump up and run if he gave her the chance.

But he merely reached under the pillow behind her, murmuring as he did so, 'Not yet, they won't, and maybe not until tonight. We have hours together before any danger of interruption.'

'I'm not letting you touch me,' Clare burst out, flailing at him with one arm, and as she did he grasped her other arm and wrenched it back above her head.

A second later she heard a metallic sound, a loud click, and felt something cold on her arm. She stared dumbly, incredulous. It was a minute before the realisation sank in.

He had handcuffed her to his wrist.

# CHAPTER EIGHT

FOR a second Clare felt a dart of fear, and then, in reaction, temper rocketed through her. 'Get these off me!' she yelled at him, and he laughed.

'Where have I heard that before?'

Scarlet, she glared. 'That was different; I've explained why I had to... oh, don't be childish. Tit for tat is just silly. Give me that key before I lose my temper.'

He had it in his free hand; smiling at her, his grey eyes light with mockery, held it out towards her then as she reached for it he threw it across the room. It hit the door and bounced off, slithered under a chest of drawers against the wall.

Clare gave a cry of fury. 'Oh, you stupid man!' She started to jump off the bed to get the key but Denzil was a dead weight; she couldn't go without him and she couldn't move him; he just lay there, gazing at her blandly while she unavailingly tugged and pulled at him.

'You'll hurt yourself if you keep doing that,' he advised.

'Oh, shut up!'

'And you won't get anywhere. Not without me, anyway, and I have no intention of moving. I'm staying right where I am, and so are you.'

Breathless and furious, Clare sat up on the edge of the bed, her back to him, trying to think what

171

to do. She should have anticipated something like this—oh, how could she have been so careless as to leave the handcuffs, not to mention the keys, around for him to get his hands on? She had been so desperate to get away last night that she had rushed off without thinking, and with a man like Denzil it was dangerous not to cover every angle of a situation. Any mistakes you made, any gaps you left he was certain to take advantage of!

Denzil's free hand began to wander up her back, sending shivers down her spine.

'Don't!'

He gave a sudden yank on the handcuffs and pulled her off balance. As she helplessly tumbled backwards Denzil's free hand closed on her waist and pulled her down on her back.

Clare gave a wordless cry of protest, looking up, eyes wide with shock, into the face bending over her.

'Now,' he said softly, 'where were we last night before you decided you had to go?'

She descended to childish pleading, stammering the words out, 'P-Please d-don't...'

'Don't tell me you're scared,' he said with a hard, sardonic smile. 'Not you, Clare! Not the woman who could play with me the way you did last night. I said your sister couldn't act, but, my God, you can! I've lost count of the parts you've played for me! The ice goddess, the tough businesswoman, the fond daughter and sister, the good housekeeper, and last night...' He paused, gave her an icy, mocking stare. 'What exactly was the part you were playing last night, Clare?'

She swallowed.

He smiled again, and her blood ran cold.

'Or weren't you acting, Clare?' Half hidden, his grey eyes gleamed between their lashes and she was terrified.

'Yes,' she said in sudden inspiration, seeing a way out. 'Of course I was acting! That's exactly what I was doing; I was...' She struggled to think of some plausible explanation. 'I was teaching you a lesson!' she finally said, and, after all, there was some truth in that. She had told herself at the time that that was what she was doing—showing him how it felt to be helpless. She gave him a direct, cool stare. 'Your victims never got the chance, but it was time someone showed you how it felt to be used and then dropped!'

He had stopped smiling. The anger in his face unnerved her. When Denzil was angry he could be alarming. 'I've told you,' he snapped. 'I didn't use anyone! And stop talking about victims—you make me sound like a serial killer!'

'Helen——' she began, and he cut her off with an impatient gesture.

'I've already explained about Helen. Why do you keep coming back to the same point? When I met her she was in the depths of despair over her divorce, and she latched on to me because I was a newcomer, someone who didn't know her or her husband. I was a new audience, if you like. She could pour out all her troubles to me, and she knew I couldn't gossip because I hardly knew a living soul in Greenhowe when I first arrived.'

'I believe all that,' Clare said in a chilly tone. 'But don't tell me you never made love to her!'

He gave her a dry glance. 'She's beautiful, I fancied her in the beginning, I may have kissed her a few times, but somehow it was hard to make love to a woman who never stopped talking about her husband. We never went to bed, if that's what you're really asking.'

Clare still didn't believe him. Angrily she asked, 'Are you saying she lied to me when she said she had been obsessed with you?'

He shrugged irritably. 'I don't know what she said to you, and I have no real idea what her feelings were, Clare; I can only speak for my own. I was never in love with Helen, and I never went to bed with her.'

She couldn't help believing him. The terse irritation in his face was very convincing, especially when he closed his eyes, sighing. 'Are you going to demand an itemised list of all the women in my life, and what I did to them?'

Crossly she said, 'No, of course not, but you can't be surprised if I had the impression you were the manipulative type—it wasn't just Helen, there was Lucy, and Bella whatever-her-name-is . . .'

'Bella has had a tragic life, but none of it was my fault. On the contrary, I gave her the chance to pull herself back from the brink, not once but several times. I gave her a part in my film that made her a big star for the first time, and I fought to get her off drugs, but you can't help people who don't want to be helped. Bella hates herself and she hates life. She has a death wish. She was ruined long before I met her.' He looked down into Clare's eyes angrily. 'I told you all this before...'

She nodded. 'I remember, but...'

'But you didn't believe me?' His voice was deep, harsh. 'I can't make you. If you don't, you don't.'

She was stricken by the look on his face and impulsively put a hand on his shoulder. 'I'm sorry, I do believe you.'

He still looked angry. 'Then why ask me again?'

'I don't know,' she wailed, biting her lip. 'I'm not thinking very straight where you're concerned.'

He frowned, his mouth indenting. 'You mean you have a fixed idea of me and however many times I explain that you got it wrong in the first place you still see me as some sort of...what was it you called me the other day? An emotional vampire?'

Clare winced. 'Yes. I'm sorry. I suppose it was just the way I met you—that night I took you and Helen to see Dark Tarn. She seemed so odd. In fact, at first I thought she was on drugs—her eyes were drowsy and yet much too bright, and then I realised she was hooked on you, not drugs. I assumed you were lovers, but Helen wasn't happy, and over the next few months she got worse and worse. She seemed to be pining away for you, getting paler and thinner, more and more frail, until she actually fainted in the street.'

'And you immediately put the blame on me!'

Flushed, she said, 'Well, what else was I to think when Helen herself definitely gave me the impression that she was unhappy over you?'

'Like most women she finds it hard to tell the plain truth about anything,' Denzil said with bitterness. 'She didn't want to admit she wanted her husband back; she thought he no longer loved her and she was too proud to let him know she still loved him. She used me as an excuse; I was her emotional alibi. If anyone asked why she looked like death, she hinted that she was in love with me.' His mouth was fierce, the force of his temper barely reined behind it. 'If anyone was used, I was! And before you get on to the subject of your sister, I never laid a finger on her!'

'Not yet, anyway,' Clare said, and he snarled back at her,

'Are you seriously accusing me of chasing that pretty little doll? You must be crazy. The only woman I've been chasing since I came to Greenhowe was you!'

Her breath almost stopped. She stared at him, white, shaking her head. 'You haven't been chasing me!'

'I tried to, but whenever I showed up you slammed the door in my face. I didn't give up for a while; I rang you, came to your office, tried to date you—and then you told me you were seriously involved with another man.'

She looked startled, then remembered what she had told him and turned carnation-pink again. 'Oh. Johnny...'

He looked into her eyes with a watchful intensity. 'Yes, Pritchard. I didn't know who you meant at first, but then I casually asked Lucy who your friend Johnny was, and she immediately told me that you were seeing my solicitor, and laughed about it, said he was a dead bore but you seemed to be crazy about him. Of course, I knew Pritchard, and I agreed with Lucy's opinion of him, but there's no accounting for taste and women like the oddest men.'

'Johnny has a lot going for him!' defended Clare crossly. 'He's charming and warm-hearted and very nice-looking...'

'Kind to animals and good to his mother. Yes, I know. I said, I've met him—and his mother, too, by the way, who seems to be a close relation of the gorgon Medusa. I doubt if she would welcome you to the family.'

Triumphantly Clare tilted her chin. 'She likes me, actually. She has known me most of my life. She didn't like Johnny's ex-wife—in fact, I think his mother helped break that up—but she has always liked me, and I like Johnny too.'

'But you lied when you told me it was serious,' he said coolly, and she bristled.

'Who says?'

'I do,' he bit out, and then his free hand leapt up and caught her chin, tilted it backwards while he leant over her, his leg imprisoning hers, his body pressing her down into the bed. Clare tried to wrench her chin free but he had too firm a grip. He looked into her wide, alarmed blue eyes.

'You would never have made love to me the way you did last night if you were in love with another man, Clare,' he said very softly, and hot colour ran up to her hairline.

'You can't be sure about that! You yourself just said I could act!'

He laughed. 'That was not acting last night, Clare.'

'You don't know me!' she said with a touch of desperation.

'I know you better than you think I do. All these weeks I've been working with your sister I've been learning everything I could about you. Oh, Lucy mostly talks about herself, but she couldn't mention herself without talking about her family, including you. I picked up a lot about you, from the books you read to what you like for breakfast.' His eyes glinted. 'She even told me you'd been watching videos of my films over and over again.'

Clare went red, said crossly, 'Well, I was curious about you, because I was worried about...about Lucy...and I thought your films might tell me what sort of man you really are and how far I could trust you, or not.'

'And did they?' he drawled.

'I learnt a lot.' She made her tone remote.

'But what did you learn?' he softly teased, and her heart skipped a beat. 'And, come to that, what did you think of my films? Did you enjoy them, while you were watching them over and over again?'

'Th—they're very good,' she stammered.

Even more softly he whispered, 'Was that where you got your ideas?'

'What?' She was suddenly scarlet, her mouth dry; she couldn't hold his gaze and because he wouldn't let her turn her head away she did the next best thing—she closed her eyes. 'I don't know what you're talking about.'

'Oh, yes, you do—that was a very erotic scene you played for me last night. Don't tell me you weren't inspired by my films.'

She gave an appalled groan. She hadn't thought of that before but now she realised that watching his films had buried those images in her unconscious, where they had got mixed up with her feelings for Denzil and charged them with a new power, a wild eroticism, which had surged out of her the instant she began to touch him last night on this bed.

'Or has your past love-life been spectacular?' Denzil asked, his fingers wandering down her throat.

'Like yours, you mean?' she bit out with a jealousy she couldn't hide.

'My love-life has always taken second place to my work, Clare,' he murmured, his hand moving caressingly down between her breasts.

'Don't,' she said, pushing his hand away.

'I never had time to meet anyone outside work. When I was making a film I would meet someone I liked a lot, and think that I was going to fall in love, but then the film I was making would be finished and I would move on, and so would she, to another film, we would see less and less of each other, and sooner or later the relationship would break up. That's the way it happens in our business.'

She had been so intent on what he was telling her that she hadn't noticed what he was doing while he talked. It was only when he paused that it dawned on her that her blouse was undone and Denzil's fingers were moving down to the belt on her skirt.

'Stop that!' She slapped his hand away and began to do up her buttons again, but as she began doing that Denzil managed to unbuckle her belt. Clare felt her skirt sliding down and gave a furious gasp, grabbing for it.

The trouble was that she only had one free hand, and she was fighting a losing battle. Denzil didn't seem to find having one hand shackled any problem at all, damn him. He was deft and supple, moving against her like an eel, far too fast for her to keep up with him.

'You didn't answer my question, Clare. Tell me about your love-life.'

'You probably know all about it already, from Lucy.' What was the point of lying now? No doubt Lucy had been horribly frank on the subject of her sister's boring love-life. 'It hasn't been mind-blowingly exciting,' she admitted, and he smiled at her.

'Neither has mine. After my childhood I was too cagey to take risks.'

Clare sighed. 'Love is risky, isn't it? I know what you mean; I've only once been in love, and then I got hurt.'

His eyes were intent. 'This was the guy I caught trying to make a heavy pass during your Christmas Eve party?'

She nodded.

'So you were in love with him once,' he said slowly.

'I thought I was for a while, but actually I realised afterwards that I never really committed myself to Hal. I had other priorities at the time—my family, the boys, my father; they needed me more than I thought Hal did, and I shouldn't have been surprised when he went off with someone else. She probably gave him what I didn't. Every relationship is a two-way street; people expect to get back what they give. I wasn't giving Hal what he wanted, so he looked elsewhere for it.'

Denzil's mouth was crooked, his glance shrewd, comprehending. 'You sound such a cool customer, Clare, you baffled me for a while, but last night I realised you weren't as cool as you pretended to be.'

Flushed, she avoided his eye. 'I suppose none of us is!'

'True,' he agreed with dry amusement. 'All my life I've waited to find someone I was sure I could trust, but because I didn't trust anybody people were often afraid of me and that made me even more suspicious of them. My relationships were never equal. Either the girl made herself a doormat, and I despised her, or I made myself a woman's best friend and although she used me as a shoulder to cry on she despised me for it.'

'You seem to me to know Helen and Lucy very well,' Clare said drily. 'And you claim to know me, too.'

He laughed curtly. 'My relationship with Helen and Lucy was pretty typical of all my relationships with women so far. I have always been curious about the way women think... I liked to listen to them talking, liked to get them talking about themselves, their feelings, what they wanted out of life; I kept hoping I would get inside their heads and really understand them, but I never did; I never understood them the way I understood men. I suppose men never understand women—our brains as well as our bodies are too different.'

'What nonsense!' Clare said crossly, pushing his hand away again. 'And will you stop trying to undress me?'

'You aren't going to tell me men and women are identical, are you, Clare?'

'No, of course we're different, but...' Clare stopped, gave a sharp cry, 'Oh!' as she felt her bra clasp give, and her smooth flesh spill out.

'"*Vive la différence*"...' Denzil said on a husky, urgent note and then his mouth was burrowing between her naked breasts and he was on top of her again, kicking his pyjama trousers off. She barely heard the smothered words he was groaning into her body. 'Oh, Clare...my God, I want you; I've spent most of the night fantasising about having you—you left me so frustrated I couldn't sleep.'

She couldn't hide a faint, fleeting smile; he looked grimly at her.

'Oh, you think that's funny, do you? I can't think of anything you could have done that could hurt more.'

She stopped smiling, went pale. 'I'm sorry.' His face worried her: he looked so angry; she shivered.

'It was cruel,' he said, his eyes hard and glittering. 'When I think...all these months, you've puzzled me, I've spent a lot of time trying to work you out, but I never dreamt you had all that passion locked inside you, and when you started making love to me I thought at last...at last she's mine...and then you climaxed, and before I knew what was going on you'd gone, leaving me in a desperate state. I didn't sleep for hours, but you're going to make up for it now, and don't pretend you don't want to make love, not after last night.' He looked into her eyes, his face flushed and excited. 'You do want me, don't you, Clare?'

'Yes.' The truth forced itself out of her, because the feel of his body pressing her down, his knee pushing her thighs apart, had aroused her to a peak of intensity where she could no longer lie, or pretend, or disguise her feelings. She wanted to experience that wild, high pleasure again. She needed him; she was afraid she would always need him.

Denzil groaned. 'Clare... I don't suppose I'll ever understand you—you're as mysterious to me as the moon. All I know is that you're under my skin, in my bloodstream, I can't think of anything else, and after last night I'd kill to have you in my bed.'

At that second it was as if she was dreaming, just as she had dreamt that Christmas Eve, months ago, as she had been dreaming all her life, waiting for it to happen, for this man to fall down on her out of the dark night, and take possession of her.

She arched with a sharp cry to meet him and they kissed; and only then did it occur to her that this was their first real kiss, because last night she had tormented him by refusing to let their mouths meet for longer than a second, had snatched her mouth away each time he searched for it.

Now it was Denzil in control, Denzil's mouth hot and urgent as it explored hers, his tongue inside her mouth, their lips melting into each other. He was heavy on top of her, moving restlessly against her, his thighs nudging hers, his hand busy.

She was so absorbed in the pleasure of his kiss that she let him strip her without fighting it. Her skirt had gone, he had broken the straps of her bra and chucked it aside.

Clare was half suffocating; Denzil broke off the kiss and they both lay there breathing thickly. That was when Clare realised that apart from her open blouse she was now only wearing panties.

Denzil's mouth was on hers again a second later, and he was caressing her slowly, his hand stroking down over her breasts, her small waist, the smooth round hips. When his hand slid inside her panties Clare caught her breath; his fingertips aroused her, heat and moisture dewing his fingers.

'Do you like that?' he whispered, hearing her gasps.

'Yes, oh, yes,' she groaned, pushing down against his fingers.

She felt the tension of the muscles in his shoulders, in the long, smooth line of his back as she explored it, following the deep indentation of the spine, down to his buttocks. She could hear his heart race; it was beating so fast that she almost felt it might at any moment accelerate beyond hypertension and stop, his body shake to bits against her.

She pushed her face into his neck and began to bite him passionately, while he arched, moaning her name in his throat like a cat purring.

Her panties had gone now, and she was naked, apart from her open shirt; he was totally naked, and fiercely aroused. Her nostrils quivered at the musky, very masculine scent that told her how much he wanted her; she slid her mouth down his chest, tasting him hungrily while he arched over her, giving his body to her, like the sky over the earth, protecting, dominating. Clare wrapped her legs around his, buried her face in his parted thighs, rubbing her cheek against the rough, curled hair, heard his deep groans increase, thicken, more and more urgent as her lips and tongue tormented him.

'Oh, God, Clare, you're driving me insane...no more...I must have you now,' he moaned, and caught hold of her waist with one hand, dragged her back up the bed and fell on her, breathing raggedly. Clare could scarcely breathe at all.

He took her so fiercely that she cried out, arching and trembling in shock-waves. This moment was the moment she had thought she feared from the first instant she met him; he had taken possession of her as she had told herself she was afraid he would, lying to herself, because it was what she longed for—her demon vampire lover, his mouth at her neck, his hands on her shaking body, enjoying his power over her, as she had wildly enjoyed her power over him last night.

Fear and desire were so inextricably entwined deep within her unconscious, but now she knew that this was what she wanted, was aching for, had to have.

The deep thrust of his flesh filled her and made her shudder, invaded, possessed, completed, satisfied. She met his thrusts and took him, held him inside her, while he groaned at the tight clench of her clamouring inner flesh, moist, hot, possessing him in turn. Clare had almost forgotten her own identity, or where she was, and she was scarcely aware of Denzil's identity either; she was moving in a primitive rhythm, her eyes shut against the world, her hot fact against his, their skin rubbing sensuously, their mouths parted, breathing thickly.

She was holding him down on her, her nails digging into his back in a spasm of pleasure, her body riding wildly, while Denzil drove into it, when the first high, wild cries broke out of her and she jerked into a climax so intense that the pleasure was almost agony; it was like dying. Deaf, dumb and blind, she gave herself up to the little death swallowing her and drowned in endless downward spirals of ecstasy.

As she slowly returned to life she heard the sounds Denzil was making, as helpless and agonised as her own, his face rigid, mask-like, skin taut, burning hot, his bones clenched.

He subsided, his breath erratic, and they both lay still for a long time afterwards, his body heavy on her, his face on her breast, their skin growing cold except where their bodies clung together moistly.

Slowly, he turned his head to find her mouth and kissed her passionately, cupping her cheek with one hand.

'I love you,' he said huskily.

Clare felt tears burn behind her lids. She couldn't speak.

He whispered, 'I've been crazy about you for a long, long time. That first day...in your office...you were so cool and offhand, an ice blonde, with don't-touch-me blue eyes. I took one look and thought, I'd like to see how deep the ice really goes!'

'Oh, did you?' she retorted, not surprised. Wasn't that what she had suspected?

He laughed in his throat. 'Oh, yes, I fancied you badly from the beginning, but I fell in love with you that Christmas Eve when I came to your house and saw you asleep in a chair by the fire...you opened your eyes and looked at me in a way that made my heart turn over, your beautiful hair was all over the place, you were flushed and untidy, and you looked human for the first time since I'd known you. I wanted to kiss you so badly that it kept me awake all night, thinking about it.'

'I'd been dreaming about you,' she said huskily.

His eyes widened; she heard his breath catch. 'Clare! What did you dream?'

'I can't remember,' she lied. 'But I opened my eyes, when the door opened, and there you were, and I didn't know if I was still dreaming or not—until I saw Dad and Lucy and the others behind you in the hall.' She didn't think this was the right moment to tell him she had dreamt he was a vampire; maybe she never would. She didn't think he would like it.

'I wish I'd known,' he said wryly. 'Think of all the time we've wasted.'

Clare tried to put her arms around his neck; the handcuffs jerked her arm down again. 'Can't we have these off now?' she asked him.

'We'll have to get up and look for the key,' he pointed out.

'In a minute, then,' said Clare, as reluctant as he was to interrupt their gentle halcyon pleasure. She put her chin on his shoulder and began moving her hand up and down his long, smooth spine, sighing with pleasure in the touch of him, thinking, He's mine; this powerful body is mine to touch whenever I want to, mine to take inside myself and possess.

Denzil was groaning, a tremor running through him at the intimate brush of her fingers.

He searched for her mouth blindly, eyes shut, and she opened her lips to him, whispering as they kissed, 'I love you... I knew I was going to fall in love with you the minute I saw you...'

He kissed her hard, then said, 'You hated me the instant you saw me, Clare, you made that clear.'

'I was terrified of you,' she confessed. 'Scared of loving you, getting hurt. I didn't want you to have power over me.'

'Do I?' he asked, and there was masked eagerness in his voice.

Clare gave him a secretive glance through her lashes. This was something else it would not be wise to tell him—that he already had a strong and terrible power over her. 'I love you,' she said. 'Isn't that enough for you?'

He would never guess that love was the power she feared more than anything else, she thought.

Denzil picked up her free hand and kissed the palm of it deeply, hotly, his eyes closed, his face passionate.

'You have power over me, Clare. I'm yours, all of me. If that isn't power, what is?'

# Take 4 bestselling love stories FREE

## Plus get a FREE surprise gift!

If you are looking for more titles by

# CHARLOTTE LAMB

Don't miss these fabulous stories by one of
Harlequin's great authors:

### Harlequin Presents®

| | | | |
|---|---|---|---|
| #11370 | DARK PURSUIT | $2.75 | ☐ |
| #11467 | HEART ON FIRE | $2.89 | ☐ |
| #11480 | SHOTGUN WEDDING | $2.89 | ☐ |
| #11560 | SLEEPING PARTNERS | $2.99 | ☐ |
| #11584 | FORBIDDEN FRUIT | $2.99 | ☐ |
| #11618 | DREAMING | $2.99 | ☐ |
| #11687 | WOUNDS OF PASSION | $2.99 U.S. | ☐ |
| | | $3.50 CAN. | ☐ |
| #11706 | GUILTY LOVE | $2.99 U.S. | ☐ |
| | | $3.50 CAN. | ☐ |

**The following titles are part of the Barbary Wharf series**

| | | | |
|---|---|---|---|
| #11498 | BESIEGED | $2.89 | ☐ |
| #11509 | BATTLE FOR POSSESSION | $2.89 | ☐ |
| #11530 | A SWEET ADDICTION | $2.89 | ☐ |

(limited quantities available on certain titles)

| | |
|---|---|
| **TOTAL AMOUNT** | $ |
| **POSTAGE & HANDLING** | $ |
| ($1.00 for one book, 50¢ for each additional) | |
| **APPLICABLE TAXES*** | $_____ |
| **TOTAL PAYABLE** | $_____ |

(check or money order—please do not send cash)

To order, complete this form and send it, along with a check or money order
for the total above, payable to Harlequin Books, to: **In the U.S.:** 3010 Walden
Avenue, P.O. Box 9047, Buffalo, NY 14269-9047; **In Canada:** P.O. Box 613,
Fort Erie, Ontario, L2A 5X3.

Name: _____

Address: _____ City: _____

State/Prov.: _____ Zip/Postal Code: _____

*New York residents remit applicable sales taxes.                    HCLBACK3
 Canadian residents remit applicable GST and provincial taxes.

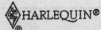